WHISKER OF A DOUBT

MYSTIC NOTCH COZY MYSTERY SERIES BOOK 6

LEIGHANN DOBBS

SUMMARY

When retired postmaster Albert Schumer is found dead on the steps of the post office, the whole town of Mystic Notch is disappointed he won't be able to play in the annual checkers tournament.

But when his ghost informs middle-aged bookstore owner Willa Chance that he died trying to deliver an old letter, which has mysteriously gone missing, Willa realizes Albert didn't just slip and fall. Someone killed him. Even worse, it turns out the letter contains a list of ingredients for a spell that could wreak havoc on Mystic Notch if it falls into the wrong hands.

The good news is that Pandora and the Mystic Notch cats are on the case. The bad news is that Pandora hasn't made much progress in getting Willa to receive her subtle communications. She's going to have to step up her game in that area because the cats are depending on her to secure the help of the humans if they want to stop the killer and protect the letter. Lucky thing Willa's love interest, Eddie Striker, seems to be more receptive to Pandora's attempt at communication.

Pandora might have a way to help the humans stop the person with the letter, earn the respect of the other cats, and help Willa and Striker realize they are made for each other. Will it work? Let's hope so, because the fate of Mystic Notch depends on it.

1

Early fall sparkled in the air around Last Chance Books as I straightened the books on the shelves. I tended to be a stickler for such things, both as a potential reader and as the bookstore's owner. Things just looked more professional that way.

As I basked in the vanilla-leather scent of old books, my two resident ghosts chattered away beside me. Normally, I did my best to ignore Robert Frost and Franklin Pierce—yes, that Robert Frost and Franklin Pierce. Despite their rather stodgy personas, they both liked to pull shenanigans on my customers. Nothing dangerous, mind you. Just little things like yanking books off the shelves. Their ghostly skills, however, were a bit limited, so I always pushed the tomes in far enough so they weren't easily scooted off by my two otherworldly companions. While I worked, I caught tidbits of their conversation, which—surprise—focused around me and telling me what I ought to be doing.

"Now, Willa," Franklin said, swirling around me in a trail of mist. "Make sure you put my biography facing outward instead of that awful Nixon chap."

I snorted but did as he asked. Nixon had been called much worse in his day, I was sure. A slight chill ran through me, as always happened when I was near an apparition. I positioned Franklin's book then gestured for him to check my placement.

"Thank you, Willa. I like that particular biography. Paints me in a rather flattering light, unlike some of the other printed rubbish." He gave a dismissive wave with his airy hand. "Oh, speaking of light, did I mention there was a disturbance of light on the ethereal plane?"

Those words stopped me short. An ominous feeling niggled my gut. Any type of disturbance on the ethereal plane was never a good sign. "No."

"It's true," Robert chimed in, glancing past me to give Franklin a knowing look. "And you know what that means."

"No," I said, wiping my now-sweaty palms on the

legs of my jeans. "I don't know. Will someone please explain?"

I was what one might call a newbie to the magical side of the world. Though I'd grown up in Mystic Notch—a magical hotbed in the gorgeous White Mountain area of New Hampshire—I'd never been a believer, at least until I'd been in a car accident that had left me with an annoying recurring pain in one leg and a persistent knack for seeing ghosts. They came to see me, talk to me, have me do things for them. Like these two with me today, except, well, they felt Last Chance Books was their home and I was just visiting.

Franklin reached out to place his hand on my shoulder, though it simply passed right through, leaving an icy trail of dread in its wake. He leaned in, his dark preternatural eyes intense. "Murder."

I gasped. No, not murder. I didn't want to get involved in another murder. Murders were problematic for me, especially since ghosts were prone to haunting me until I solved theirs. I had no idea why they came to me. It was like there was some sort of invisible sign over my head.

Feeling shaken, I went to the front counter and started stacking the books I'd purchased at an estate sale earlier in the week next to the antique cash register.

"That's ridiculous," I said, thankful there were no customers in the store. We didn't open for another hour. Right now, I felt flustered and hot and totally discombobulated by Franklin's pronouncement. "How could you possibly know that?"

Robert floated over to lean a ghostly hip against the counter while I fiddled with counting the drawer. "Well, being a ghost gives us certain insights into things. Normally, the kind of disturbance we felt last night is due to a spirit whose life has been taken by another. They show up in the ethereal plane completely shocked, unprepared for their mortal lives to be over, many times angry, and always confused. Doesn't take a rocket scientist to spot a victim who's been murdered."

A shudder ran through me before I could stop it. "Please tell me this doesn't mean another ghost is going to start haunting me, wanting me to help solve the mystery. With the holiday season approaching, I really don't have time for investigations right now."

The first time one of them had visited me after my accident, I'd thought I'd gone insane. But then it started happening more and more. Now, seeing dead people was nearly routine. I'd learned to deal with it and wouldn't have minded, except that these new ghosts were so needy. They seemed to be reaching new levels of insistence that I help them. In other words, they wouldn't take no for an answer.

"This ghost is rather shy," Franklin said, drifting over to stand on my other side. "I'm not surprised he hasn't made his presence known to you yet. But you know the rules, Willa. If you don't help them solve their mystery, the poor creature will be stuck in Limbo forever. Very distressing."

The church bells rang at eight o'clock sharp, and I walked to the front door of the bookstore to open the shop. The large oak door swung open to reveal my morning regulars waiting outside. Cordelia and Hattie Deering, twin ladies in their early eighties, looked as dashing as always in their almost-matching polyester pantsuits—Cordelia's was tan with a black turtleneck beneath, and Hattie's was black with a tan turtleneck. Bing Thorndike followed behind them with a tray of hot teas and coffees for them all. Josiah Barrows brought up the rear. Josiah was Mystic Notch's retired postmaster, and Bing was an ex-magician.

"Ah, Willa, dear," Bing said, his mischievous blue eyes sparkling beneath his bushy white eyebrows. "Good morning. Here's your coffee."

I took the white Styrofoam cup from him and

sipped at the hot brew while everyone settled in the comfy seating area of the shop. I'd put in a purple micro-suede couch and a couple of matching armchairs in the hopes of giving the place a homier feel after I'd taken over for my late grandmother. The seating was a big hit with my regulars. I took a seat at the end of the sofa, leaving Franklin and Robert to hover around the cash register. I figured they'd soon disappear back to wherever it was they came from. I was the only one that could see them, and they got bored when I ignored them to talk to flesh-and-blood beings.

When I'd lived down in Massachusetts, if anyone had told me I'd own a bookstore and be a ghost whisperer one day, I'd have laughed in their faces. Guess fate was the one laughing now.

I'd just settled in when my cat, Pandora, walked over and plopped down atop my feet. With sleek gray fur and mesmerizing golden-green eyes, she did her mythical namesake proud. She watched all of us intently, turning her head this way and that as if she understood what we were saying. I'd inherited Pandora along with the bookstore and a house from my grandmother, and until recently, I'd figured she was a typical feline, aloof and self-possessed.

After what had happened earlier this summer,

though, I'd started to wonder about Pandora. I'd been trapped in a fire, and though I couldn't remember much of what had happened, I somehow got the impression Pandora had had a more-than-catlike role in saving me. Sometimes, I'd get these thoughts, like she was communicating telepathically with me or something—tidbits of information or suggestions or, in the case of the fire, downright warnings. The thing was, they were never wrong. Odd, really, any way I looked at it.

"My dear, have you heard about poor Iona at the Cut and Curl?" Hattie asked me.

My gut clenched. Was Iona the one who'd been murdered? The thought of the hyperactive hairdresser haunting me made me nervous. "No," I squeaked out past the lump in my throat then slurped my coffee nervously. For octogenarians, these ladies sure had their fingers on the pulse of what was happening in Mystic Notch. "What happened?"

"She left her husband. That's what," Cordelia said, her voice lowered to a conspiratorial whisper. "Shameful if you ask me. I'd bet good money she's run off with that philandering new mechanic at the garage."

Relief swept over me. Iona wasn't dead. Not only that, but if there'd been a murder in our tiny little town, these two would certainly know. Apparently, Robert and Franklin were wrong. I glanced in the direction of the cash register, but they were gone. Probably off trying to figure out how they'd gotten their spirit radar messed up.

While Bing engaged the ladies in more tawdry gossip about Iona, I turned to Josiah, who looked a bit down in the dumps. "What's wrong? You look like you lost your best friend."

He shrugged. "Nah. It's just that the annual postmasters' checkers tournament is this Friday."

"That's a good thing, though, right?" I asked.

"Should be," Cordelia said. "You look forward to that every year, Josiah."

"I do." His shoulders slumped. "This year will be a bit sad, though."

"Why?" Bing frowned.

That unease I'd felt earlier returned, knotting my stomach. Josiah didn't just look like he'd lost a friend —he looked like a friend had died. But if someone he knew had been murdered, surely he would have mentioned it sooner. He wouldn't just be sitting there, not saying a word about it. Murder was big news in Mystic Notch.

Okay, well, it used to be big news, but according to my sister, Augusta, who was the county sheriff, there had been a lot more murders since I had moved back to town. I was sure that was just an odd coincidence.

"Albert Schumer was the best player in three counties. I loved the challenge of going up against him every year. Kept my skills sharp." Josiah's voice sounded sad, and my heart sank. He'd said "was," not "is." Past tense.

Bing and the ladies all nodded in agreement with Josiah's assessment of another of Mystic Notch's former postmasters.

"Will he not be attending this year?" Hattie asked, concerned and more than a tad nosy.

"You haven't heard?" Josiah looked up at us, his brows knit.

We all shook our heads, and my breath seized in my lungs as I waited for that shoe to drop.

"Albert won't be playing checkers ever again. He was found dead on the back steps of the post office early this morning."

Pandora let out a ghastly meow, and my gaze flew to where Robert and Franklin had reappeared near the register, satisfied looks on their ghostly faces. Warning bells clanged loudly in my head. It was true.

There'd been another murder in quiet little Mystic Notch.

2

By midafternoon, my leg was killing me, and there'd been no sign of Albert's ghost. Maybe Robert and Franklin *were* mistaken. I'd heard no news that Albert Schumer had been murdered. In fact, from what I'd gathered from my customers that day, the scuttlebutt around town was that he'd fallen and hit his head. There was also some question of a possible heart attack involved. But no rumors of *murder*. Yet.

Afternoons in Mystic Notch were slow, which was a nice respite following the generally busy mornings. Most days, my best friend, Pepper St. Onge—who owned The Tea Shoppe down the street—stopped in for a snack and a chat, since neither one of us usually took a proper lunch. Today was no exception.

Pepper showed up around three p.m. with her

special quilted green-and-pink tea cozy in hand. She was a striking woman, with long red hair piled on top of her head and bright-emerald eyes. Known for her cute fashion sense, Pepper had on a peach twinset and a pastel wool plaid skirt to keep her warm against the gathering autumn chill. She looked cute in a vintage kind of way and a lot younger than her forty-eight years.

"Hi, Willa," Pepper said as she entered the bookstore, the bells jangling merrily at her arrival. I was so glad to have a friend like Pepper in town. I'd known her forever. We'd been best friends since kindergarten. We'd grown apart a little when I left town for college but picked up again when I returned as if no time had passed. I could tell Pepper anything. In fact, she was the only person that knew I could talk to ghosts, and it sure was a relief to talk to her about it.

She walked over to the vacant seating area and began to unpack her mysteriously never-ending tea cozy. She'd made it herself specifically to carry her special teas and accompaniments. She could store an entire tea service in there, and I watched, fascinated, as she pulled out a silver teapot, dainty floral china teacups and saucers, embroidered linen napkins, a matching silver sugar bowl and creamer, and even a plate of scones.

She looked up at me and smiled. "How's it going?"

"Fine, except for what happened to poor Albert Schumer." I took a seat in one of the armchairs, watching as Pepper set things up on the coffee table. I enjoyed these talks more than I enjoyed her tea, truth be told.

There were times when I felt... *funny*... after drinking it. Not ill, per se, but more like *suggestible.* Pepper claimed that her teas had a special kind of magic, one that could heal and make wishes come true. Of course, Pepper said she never put anything in the teas unless someone wanted her to. I wasn't sure if I quite believed the teas were charmed or magical because it seemed to me that whatever she thought her tea was supposed to accomplish backfired more often than not. Truth be told, I was a bit of a nonbeliever in magic. Some might say that was odd, given my undead visitors, but I considered them a weird side effect of my accident—one I hoped would vanish one day—definitely not due to magical powers of any kind.

"Oh, I heard about that," Pepper said, pushing the plate piled high with homemade butter brickle scones toward me. Pepper settled herself primly on the edge of the sofa then poured us each a cup of tea and placed a scone on a delicate pink napkin for me. "Such awful news. Apparently, Ruthie's the one who found him dead on the back steps when she went to open up for the day."

Ruthie Michaels was the current postmaster of Mystic Notch and about as nonthreatening as they came. Seeing Albert's crumpled body must've given her quite a fright. "I wonder why he was using the back entrance," I said, sipping my yummy mandarin spice tea. "I mean, I know the current employees use that back door, but I didn't figure the retired ones would."

"Oh, I don't think it's that unusual." Pepper nibbled one of her delicious scones. Her baked goods were nearly as popular with the tourists as the homemade herbal teas she sold. I took a large bite of mine too, enjoying the chewy pastry and the sweet toffee crunch of the butter brickle chips. Pepper dabbed her mouth with her napkin before continuing. "A lot of the employees there, past and present, still hang out around the back entrance, from what I've seen."

"Robert and Franklin told me about a disturbance in the light on the other side in the wee hours this morning." I glanced around to make sure neither ghost was present at the moment. Coast clear, I leaned a bit closer to Pepper to whisper, "They suspected a murder."

"Goodness." Pepper paused mid-sip, her green eyes wide. "You don't think—"

"At first, yes. I've been waiting for poor Albert to show up in my store all day." I gave a shudder. "But no show so far, thank heavens." I straightened and sighed. "The fellows must've been mistaken this time."

"Hmm." Pepper continued to watch me over the rim of her cup as Pandora strolled over to twine herself around my ankles. "For your sake, I hope so."

Pandora moved from me to Pepper, meowing loudly.

"Would you like some cream?" Pepper asked, speaking directly to the cat as if she could understand her.

Pandora meowed again, this time more quietly, and the two of them proceeded to have a conversation, with Pepper talking and cooing and Pandora meowing and purring. Pepper poured some cream from her sterling-silver creamer into a delicate porcelain saucer rimmed with tiny blue flowers. Pepper seemed quite serious about the conversation. Pandora seemed more serious about the cream.

Pepper put down the saucer for Pandora then turned back to me, as if realizing I was still there. She smiled, a slow affair, brimming with secrets I wasn't privy to. Did she actually think she'd been communicating with my cat? Then again, I'd begun to wonder if Pandora wasn't smarter than the average cat. Not for the first time since I'd returned to Mystic Notch, I wondered how I'd ever managed to leave this place in the beginning and how I was ever going to blend in again now that I was back.

"So, do you think Albert might still show up?" Pepper asked. "Rumor around town is his heart gave out."

"Not sure." I finished my tea and scone then set my dishes back on the small table between us. "I hope not. If he does, I'll know for sure it was murder. Robert and Franklin both described Albert as shy, though, so it may take him some time to make himself visible."

I shifted in my seat then winced as familiar pain seared up my left leg. The bones had been shattered during the accident, and now, after multiple surgeries and metal pins to put me back together, the stiffness never quite went away. We spent the next few minutes discussing the other goings-on around town—the new gift shop selling all kinds of tacky souvenirs for the tourists, the rumors about Iona leaving her husband, the early chill, and our mutual hopes that this year's winter would be mild instead of the snowy mess we'd had in previous years. The tourists loved the skiing, but ice and blocked roads didn't bode well for the local business community.

"Leg bothering you again?" Pepper reached into her cozy again and pulled out a bag of tea. "Try this. It's dandelion. Works wonders for arthritis and joint issues."

"Thanks." I took the plastic bag then creaked to my feet to help her pack up and dispose of our trash. "And thanks for the tea and scones. It really hit the spot today."

"You're welcome," Pepper said, placing her repacked cozy over her arm then heading for the door. "Keep me posted on what happens with Albert."

"Will do." I waved as she left the shop, then turned back to find Pandora up on the table, sniffing the bag of tea Pepper had left me. Her sleek gray tail waved high in the air, the kinked end making it look like an angular question mark. Pandora gave a final sniff then looked up at me with her wise golden-green eyes and meowed loudly.

3

Albert's ghost still hadn't shown up by the time I closed the store at five, so I called my sister. If anyone would know about a murder taking place in town, it would be Gus. Never mind she didn't like me poking around in her investigations and probably wouldn't tell me about official law enforcement business anyway. I'd still at least get a clue by gauging her level of hostility toward my question when I mentioned it.

I gathered my purse and Pandora then locked up the bookstore, dialing with my free hand as I walked to my Jeep. After climbing inside the vehicle, I started the engine and connected the phone to Bluetooth before pulling away from the curb.

"Sheriff Augusta Chance," Gus answered the call, her tone as crisp and professional as always.

"Hey, it's Willa," I said, keeping my gaze straight ahead as I slowly passed through the quaint, crowded downtown area.

"I hope you're not using your phone while driving." Gus's disapproving frown was evident in her voice. "That's illegal in this state."

"I know that." I slowed for a red light and glanced over at Pandora, who was curled up sleeping, on the passenger seat. "I'm using Bluetooth. So, how's your day going?"

"Fine." Suspicion mingled with the disapproval now. Gus and I got along well enough but weren't super close. I tended to be more open to new ideas and ways of doing things, while Gus was pretty set in her ways. And all the magical talk around Mystic Notch? Forget it. She wouldn't even listen.

Needless to say, I'd not mentioned my new postaccident abilities to her at all. She'd probably lock me up in a looney bin somewhere. So, when one of my ghostly visitors demanded I poke my nose into one of Gus's murder investigations, I had to fib a bit. Thus, my sister considered me a nosy nuisance, telling me I must watch too many crime shows on TV or something.

"Look, I appreciate the courtesy call, but unless you've got important business, sis, I'm going to have to go. Things are swamped round here today."

"Oh yeah?" I asked, seizing the opportunity. "Why's that? Wouldn't have anything to do with what happened to poor old Albert Schumer, would it?"

Gus hesitated, and my interest soared. "What do you know about Albert Schumer?"

"Just that Josiah Barrows was in this morning for coffee and he mentioned poor Albert died last night. I wondered if there was anything... *odd* about his demise."

"Odd?" Gus exhaled loudly through the phone line. "Look, Willa. I've told you before, I don't like you sticking your nose into these cases. It's dangerous and just plain weird. I'm treating what happened to Albert like I would any other deceased person found on public property. End of story."

I turned onto the quiet, picturesque side street where the large Victorian I'd inherited from my grandmother was located, my tense shoulders relaxing slightly. All these big trees and tidy yards gave me a sense of peace I'd missed while living in the big city.

"Okay. I'm not pushing here. Don't get all defensive." I turned into my driveway and parked. "I was just asking."

"Have you checked on Elspeth yet today?" Gus asked, switching topics. "I've been so busy I haven't had time."

"No. You want me to drive over there now to see her?" It wasn't that far, and the evening was warm for fall. It seemed a shame to go inside just yet. "It's no problem at all."

"If you could, that'd be great," Gus said. "I gotta go."

"Talk to you later, sis."

"Later."

Elspeth had been a good friend of my late grandmother's, and Gus and I had both promised Gram we'd check on the elderly lady regularly to make sure she was all right. There was a path through the woods behind my house that connected our two properties, and considering I'd spent most of the day doing paperwork or reshelving books, the exercise would do me good.

"C'mon, Pandora. Let's get you some dinner, then we'll go over and see Elspeth."

The cat shot out of the vehicle as soon as I opened my door, and stood on the porch waiting for me. It was past her dinnertime, and she was none too happy about it either, if the flat stare she gave me was any indication.

I gathered my things, locked the car, then limped up to the side porch, where I usually entered. The huge one-hundred-fifty-year-old Victorian home was too big for one person, really—with three stories, two living rooms, and five bedrooms—but that hadn't stopped me from keeping it. It had belonged to my dear grandmother, and I loved every inch of its thirty-five hundred square feet, with its black-and-white shutters, sprawling property—now covered with brightly colored fall leaves—and stretches of white fence marking the borders.

Near the back of the area, about five hundred feet or so from the main house, sat a large red-and-white barn that used to house a stable. At one time, if I remembered correctly, Gram had kept horses. Inside the barn, I could still smell old leather from the saddles, hay, and manure. If the breeze was just right, I'd even catch the phantom whinny of a long-gone mare, and I could still see the teeth marks on the stall doors where the horses had chewed the wood. I loved the place. Maybe someday, I'd save up enough money to keep a horse of my own there.

My stomach growled as I unlocked the house door and let us in. Shadows from the two turrets on either side of the house lengthened as the sun began to set. The wooden porch creaked beneath my feet.

"Come on, girl. Let's get inside and get you some food, eh?"

Pandora meowed loudly again.

After fixing the cat a bowl of chow, I peeked into the fridge for a snack. Good thing Striker was coming over later and bringing takeout. I hadn't had a chance to go to the grocery store yet, and pickings were slim.

While Pandora devoured her meal, I settled on a handful of olives. I'd not seen Eddie Striker for about a week. He was the sheriff of the next county over—Dixford Pass—and my on-again, off-again boyfriend. We were taking things slowly, neither wanting to rush into anything, and it was nice. More than nice, actually. Striker was sweet and kind and made thoughtful gestures, like bringing me dinner tonight. Not to mention, he was good-looking—tall, dark, broad shouldered. And I'd always been a sucker for gray eyes. He'd be here in about an hour, so I needed to make my trip to check on Elspeth fast.

Once Pandora finished eating, we headed out the back door and down the path through the woods. Chipmunks scurried through the dried leaves on the ground, and birds tweeted from the tall trees around us in the dwindling light. The scene was quiet and peaceful, and I caught the scent of cookies baking before we even reached Elspeth's house.

A feeling of familiar comfort came over me as I emerged from the trees on the other side of the small forest and saw a light-green Victorian home with pink gingerbread detail. I had fond memories of visiting Elspeth with Gram when I was a little girl. We walked up onto the porch. The white railings of the wrap-around porch were still covered with gorgeous pink roses, which were unusual to still be blooming this time of year, but Elspeth had a magical touch with plants.

On the porch, one of Elspeth's many cats, an orange tomcat named Tigger, rose to meet Pandora. They both sniffed each other in greeting then trotted off toward Elspeth's barn as if they had very important business to discuss.

I smiled and shook my head then knocked briefly on the screen door. The wooden door was open, and I peered in through the screen at the living room. "Elspeth? It's Willa."

"Oh, Willa dear. Please come in," Elspeth called. "I'm in the kitchen."

Following the scent of cookies, I walked into her spacious, old-country kitchen. There were cookies cooling on racks covering all the counters and even the large butcher-block island in the center of the space. I laughed. "Looks like you've baked enough for the entire town here."

"Evie Hamilton was over earlier today, and we were making some recipes from Betty's recipe book." She pointed toward a flour-covered tome in the center of the island. "You remember that one, don't you, Willa?"

Yep, I did. How could I forget the tattered tome that had played an odd role in finding the killer of Adelaide Hamilton? If I closed my eyes, I could still see Adelaide's ghost before me, insisting I find the cookbook and give it to Elspeth. Such a strange request.

Too bad that hadn't been the only strange thing about that visitation. Evie seemed to have some strange abilities too, if I recalled correctly. The whole thing was a bit foggy now, though. It had all ended in a terrible fire, and I'd suffered smoke inhalation. The doctor had said my memory might be a tad off from it too, which probably accounted for the crazy images I had of a bunch of cats helping me escape and someone being turned into a toad.

I frowned. There'd also been some question about the types of recipes in that cookbook, I remembered. In fact, Pepper insisted her grandmother had told her Betty's book wasn't filled with recipes at all, but instead was filled with spells. I blinked hard. Why would Elspeth have a spell book? But of course, it wasn't a spell book. The cookies cooling on the counter proved it.

"Would you like a cookie, dear?" Elspeth asked, holding out a plate.

"Oh, no, thank you. I've not had dinner yet."

"This is my second batch today," Elspeth said, putting the plate aside and heading back to her oven. "The first batch, I took over to poor Grace Schumer to pay my respects for Albert's death." She sighed. "If he wasn't such a conscientious postmaster, he might not have slipped on the steps and might still be alive right now."

My interest piqued anew, I rested my hip against the edge of the counter to relieve the ache in my leg and crossed my arms. That was a weird thing to say. Maybe Elspeth knew something about Albert Schumer's death. "What do you mean he might be alive if he wasn't so conscientious? I thought he slipped or had a heart attack."

Elspeth looked at me sharply. "Yes, that's what they say. Did you hear otherwise?"

"No, but what does that have to do with him being conscientious?"

"Oh, well, Grace told me that Albert found an old

piece of undelivered mail in his belongings from when he was a postmaster. I guess it got lodged in one of the old postal bags he used to carry, and never got delivered. He felt determined to see it delivered to its rightful owner, and if he hadn't gone right off to the post office that minute, he might not have slipped on the steps."

"Well, if it was from that long ago, I can't imagine the person would still be alive."

Elspeth shrugged. "That's not the point, dear. To a postmaster, the mail must be delivered. They take an oath and everything."

"Hmm." I glanced at the clock above the stove and realized Striker would be arriving in about ten minutes. "Could I take some cookies home with me for dessert?"

"Of course, dear." Elspeth boxed up about a dozen for me then walked me back to the front door. "Thank you for checking in on me, Willa."

"My pleasure." I kissed her on the cheek then headed back outside. Pandora was nowhere to be seen. I called for her, but she didn't come out, so I started back down the path toward my house. The cat had lived here longer than I had and could take care of herself. She always caught up with me in the end.

As I walked back through the twilight woods, I

kept my eye out for Albert's ghost, hoping he might pop up along the way, but no such luck. Hard to believe a letter that old would just turn up out of nowhere in someone's belongings. Funny how Josiah hadn't mentioned it that morning, nor had Gus. If there really had been a letter, as Grace had told Elspeth, then what had happened to it?

4

Elspeth's barn was dark inside, with only a few shafts of light filtering in through the small, dusty windows and from the partially open barn door. Pandora padded inside then stopped, glancing around at the bales of hay scattered about the floor and the stainless-steel bowls of cat food lined up against one wall.

The barn was home to the many cats that Elspeth had adopted over the years. But these weren't ordinary cats. They were the cats of Mystic Notch. A unique band of felines sworn to help ensure the magic in the notch stayed on the side of "good."

Pandora's eyes immediately adjusted to the dim light inside the barn, and she looked around at her comrades, some of whom had come out from their various napping spots to sit in a circle in the middle of the barn. Some stayed in the lofts, peering down on them, and others—like the fat calico Otis—were perched on top of hay bales. As Pandora had suspected, they were already discussing Albert Schumer's death.

"Well, I happen to know the Schumers' cat," Sasha said, her head raised in true regal Siamese style, her sky-blue eyes glittering. "And she said the letter Albert had was from Helen Warren, poor old Hester Warren's great-grandniece."

Snowball, a fluffy white Persian, stopped mid-lick of a paw to stare wide-eyed at Sasha. "You don't think..."

"That it has something to do with the legend?" Sasha tilted her head, her piercing blue eyes narrowed. "Hard to tell at this point, but it is possible."

"If this is linked to Hester, then his death might be important," Pandora said.

Her feline intuition had already told her that Albert's death was no accident. Judging by what Robert and Franklin had told her in the bookstore, she knew that the man had definitely been murdered. Why his ghost had not appeared to Willa was a mystery. Perhaps he really was shy. Pandora had prowled the bookstore all day, waiting for him, but to no avail.

The dandelion tea Pepper had given Willa should help.

Not only was it good for healing pain, it also helped provide a stronger connection to the spirit world. Pepper had likely known that but omitted that little tidbit to Willa, knowing how stubborn and skeptical she was. She probably would refuse to drink the tea, thinking it would cause even more ghosts to haunt her. Pandora could only hope that Albert would appear at Willa's house tonight. If not, she might have to take drastic measures because, if the letter really did have to do with the legend, then what they needed to accomplish could not be done by felines alone. They would need human help.

"No kidding." Otis glared down at her, setting Pandora's whiskers twitching. There was no love lost between her and Otis. Even though they'd teamed up once to help their cause, and even though she'd sensed that his bark was worse than his bite, Otis still couldn't stop himself from being snarky with her, and she couldn't stop herself from reacting.

She knew she should just let it go, but he really got her dander up.

Pandora didn't need to point out that they'd almost lost their battle once here in the notch when an old potion that Hester Warren had tried to protect had surfaced. She didn't need to remind them how the ghost of Hester's cat, Obsidian, had helped them. She didn't need to bring up the fact that things like this should not be taken lightly in Mystic Notch.

"If that's the case, we have to find the letter and make sure it does not fall into the hands of evil. That pleasantry charm is the only thing keeping this village civil," Tigger added, his sleek orange body tense. "To reverse it would be a catastrophe."

Pandora gave him a side-look for his bad pun then shook her head. An old feline legend said that Hester Warren had hidden a bunch of sacred ingredients around Mystic Notch prior to her trial and subsequent hanging for witchcraft. According to the story, these ingredients could be collected then used to reverse the pleasantry charm that had been cast over the town long ago.

If removed, it would allow the evildoers who'd once populated Mystic Notch to rise again, causing all sorts of nasty chaos. Arguments would erupt, neighbors would stop getting along, and fortunes would change for all when the darkness came to power. The legend also said that, before her execution, Hester wrote down the locations of all the secret ingredients and gave the document to her great-grandniece, Helen, for safekeeping.

"It's possible the letter Albert was trying to mail has the locations," Pandora said. All the cats gave a solemn nod. "Right. Then we must stop whoever took the letter from digging up these ingredients at all costs."

"Easier said than done when these humans have no clue of the doom lurking around them," Inkspot said, his deep voice resounding through the barn. He was their ring-leader and an imposing presence, with his large jet-black body and knowing yellow eyes. "What about your human, Pandora? She sees ghosts. Surely she has spoken to Albert."

"Uhh... well... not exactly." Pandora cringed. Here in the notch, some judged a cat's worth in part by her ability to control her human. "Unfortunately, Willa hasn't gotten a visit from Albert's spirit yet."

Otis snorted, giving Pandora a dismissive wave of his paw. "Even if your human had talked to the dead guy, it isn't like you could ask her anyway right, Pandora? You never could get that woman to do what you want."

The needling by her nemesis did the trick and caused Pandora to lift her head high, giving even regal Sasha a run for her money. "I can do it. Willa is coming along nicely, and it has nothing to do with her, anyway. Albert's just shy. I won't fail this time. I've got an idea."

"Glad to hear it," Otis said, sounding completely unconvinced. "Try it, then. As long as the silly humans put the person responsible for Albert's murder behind bars, then we won't have to worry about them collecting the ingredients or revealing our secret legend to them."

"In the meantime, we need to be diligent. Everyone, keep a lookout for anything suspicious, and report back

here if needed," Inkspot said. Even though his words didn't say as much, Pandora knew that his willingness for her to try her idea was a vote of confidence in her skills. Her heart warmed.

Pandora trotted out of the barn, paws crossed in her mind that her idea would work.

5

Sure enough, I'd just reached the back door of my house when Pandora caught up with me. I let us into the kitchen, put the cookies on the counter, then secured the door behind us before setting out plates and silverware and napkins. Striker would be here any minute, and my leg was killing me after the walk over to Elspeth's.

As I rummaged in the drawer for the bottle of aspirin, Pandora hopped up on the counter.

"Hey, get off there."

She knew better than to get on the counters and was usually pretty good about it, but if there was one thing I'd learned about Pandora, it was that she disliked being yelled at. She stubbornly ignored me, stuck her paw out, and batted at a little bag. The dandelion tea that Pepper had given me.

Smack, smack.

The tea bag fell on the floor. Pandora looked right at me and meowed as if to say, "I'll hop up on anything I please," then she jumped down to the floor, twitching her tail as she sauntered off to the living room.

I'd forgotten Pepper had given me the tea. She'd said it might help with my leg. Turned out Pandora had actually done me a favor.

I made myself a cup of the tea and took an aspirin. The tea wasn't too bad. I'd expected it to be bitter—like the time I'd licked the dandelion milk off my fingers after plucking the yellow flowers off the stems as a kid—but it wasn't. It was kind of earthy and not too unpleasant.

I snagged a snickerdoodle from the cookie box, took my stoneware mug of tea into the living room, and settled on the sofa to munch the cookie and check the emails on my phone while I waited for my dinner. I'd requested burgers from the diner in town if Striker didn't have a preference. They were the best I'd ever had—thick and juicy and doused in cheese and ketchup and mustard—along with the amazing fries that came with them. My stomach rumbled in anticipation.

Pandora settled on the coffee table in front of me and began batting her paw against the glass globe paperweight Elspeth had given me as a gift shortly after I'd moved back to Mystic Notch. I set my phone aside and glanced at the cat over the rim of my cup. "Don't break that. Elspeth gave it to me."

The cat meowed loudly and stared at me with her bright-emerald gaze that made me think she could see right into my soul. I sat forward to pet her head then noticed a strange glow emanating from the center of the globe. Weird. Sure, I'd seen the orb catch the sunlight sometimes and work like a prism, sending a rainbow of colors over the walls of the room, but it was night now. I frowned, leaning closer to peer through the glass, noticing more detail now—leaves, dirt, a sort of swirly, misty smoke billowing, and—oh no!

"Albert?" I whispered, my eyes wide.

Pandora meowed loudly.

The ghostly form inside the globe shimmered, quivered slightly, seemed to beckon me closer again...

Knock. Knock. Knock.

Pounding on the kitchen door jarred me from my trance. Feeling slightly disoriented, I shook my head to clear it and peered out the window into the driveway. Striker. I glanced back over at the coffee table, but the globe was back to normal. Had I imagined seeing Albert Schumer's ghost in there?

"Hey, Chance," Striker said as I let him inside. He'd taken to calling me by my last name when we first met. He said it was appropriate since I took a lot of chances. He kissed my cheek then held up the two grease-stained paper bags with a grin. "I come bearing burgers."

"Fantastic! I'm starving."

He peered into the box of cookies on the counter. "Elspeth?"

"Fresh baked today."

I led him over to where I had plates and napkins set up at the vintage kitchen table, and we dug into our food. "How was your day? Anything exciting happening in Dixford Pass?"

"Nah," Striker said around a bite of burger. He wiped a glob of mustard from his chin before continuing. "Same old, same old. Hear your sister Gus has her hands full, though, with what happened to Albert."

"Yeah." I gave another look back at the globe to be sure the ghost wasn't lingering around. Pandora took the opportunity to hop up on Striker's lap and try to get at his fries, but I shooed her away before she could nab one. She glared before she jumped down and trotted off toward the stairs like she owned the place.

Striker chuckled. "Best check your pillow tonight for hair balls."

"No kidding." I took another bite of food, savoring the charbroiled goodness of the meat while trying to shake my unease about Albert.

What if he decided to get over his shyness and show up here in my house while Striker was about? I wanted to talk to the ghost but not at the expense of my budding relationship with Striker. It's hard enough to find suitable single men to date when you're pushing fifty, let alone in such a tiny town like Mystic Notch. Plus, I was kind of stuck on Striker. I didn't want to send him running.

Striker knew nothing about my special "gift," and I intended to keep it that way forever, if possible. Still, being in law enforcement gave him access to certain information I wasn't privy to, nor could I ask Gus. I decided to pry just a bit to see what I could find out. "So, have you talked to Gus about her new case?"

"About Albert, you mean?" He devoured his last bite of burger. "No. What I've heard is probably what everyone knows from the local scuttlebutt or whatever. Your sister only calls me for help if it's a murder, anyway. And from what I've heard, Albert just slipped and fell."

"Right." I nibbled on another fry, trying to play off

my curiosity as boredom. "Well, it was interesting while it lasted."

"Yeah."

I finished my burger, and Striker started cleaning up the debris while I worked on the last of my fries. That was another thing I liked about him—not only did he bring the food, but he cleaned it up too.

"Want to watch that new movie on cable?" he asked.

"Uh, sure. Be right there." I finished the last of my fries, my mind still whirling with what I'd seen in that glass globe. Albert wouldn't have tried to contact me if there wasn't something wrong with his death, something unfinished or something that needed to be set right.

Then again, I wasn't exactly sure that swirling apparition was Albert. So far, no ghosts had tried to contact me through the paperweight. It was probably just an optical illusion. I didn't know what kind of glass that thing was made out of, but this wasn't the first time it had reflected something strange.

My mind wandered to the missing letter. I couldn't shake the feeling that the letter had something to do with Albert's death. And where was the letter now? Did Ruthie mail it? Did it blow away in the wind? Was Grace wrong about it? Or did someone take it?

My thoughts continued to whirl as I settled in beside Striker on the sofa, his arm warm around my shoulders. He passed me a cookie as I cuddled into his side. Tomorrow, I'd look into it further. Tonight, I'd enjoy my movie and my company.

6

The next morning, Pandora and I arrived at Last Chance Books to find the regulars already waiting outside, coffees in hand. I unlocked the door then gestured them all inside before setting my purse on the counter.

I'd brought some of the dandelion tea Pepper had given me from home, but right now the coffee Bing had brought for me was looking far more appealing. At least my leg was aching less this morning. Maybe the tea really did work.

I headed over to where the group was gathering in the sitting area. Behind me, Pandora patted the pocket of my purse where the tea bags were located and meowed. She was obsessed with that tea. Maybe dried dandelion was like catnip or something. Either way, I didn't want her scratching up my leather purse, so I picked her up and carried her over to the purple sofa in the sitting area with me. She looked none too happy about it and squirmed around as if it were undignified to be carried, but that was too bad. I needed caffeine this morning. I also needed to find out if the regulars had discovered anything more about Albert's death.

"Has anyone heard anything new?" I asked as nonchalantly as possible as I took a sip of my steaming-hot coffee.

"About Albert?" Hattie asked. "No. Just awful what happened."

"Yes," Cordelia agreed. They were dressed in shades of blue today—Cordelia in a navy pantsuit with a turquoise top and Hattie the opposite. "Such a terrible way to die, alone on those cold stone steps like that."

"You know, I've been thinking," Bing said, frowning. "I wonder if Albert had a stroke. That could certainly explain why he slipped and fell."

"Hmm." Cordelia shrugged. "Well, if we're putting out theories, maybe Barney Delaney did him in. He was always coming in second to Albert in that checkers tournament, and now that Albert's gone, Barney's a shoo-in to win the contest."

"No, I doubt it was Barney. He's not the type to

murder someone. Heck, he's usually jumping at his own shadow. I see him a lot at the local auctions. I go to check out the used books for the shop. You'd be surprised how many times first editions show up in box lots from local estates who don't realize what they've got. Barney's usually there to find new stock for his antique store down the street. He even comes in here sometimes, looking for obscure, out-of-print reference books to help him evaluate his antiques." I glanced over at the stack of tomes that had been delivered the day before. I'd bought them on eBay, and there were some great hard-to-find books in the pile. "I just got a bunch in too. I should let him know. I think the police should be looking into that missing letter."

"I'm still not certain there *was* a letter," Josiah said. "When I talked to Ruthie about it yesterday, she never mentioned it once. Seems it would come up, being so important and all."

"Who told you about this letter again, Willa?" Bing asked.

"Elspeth. She said Albert found it while he was going through some of his old postmaster stuff and felt it should be returned to its rightful owner after all this time."

Bing's expression turned thoughtful, and he

pushed to his feet. “Sorry, everyone, but I need to run this morning. Lots of stuff to do.”

“Yes, us too,” Hattie said, rising and pulling Cordelia up beside her. “We’ll see you tomorrow, dear.”

Josiah stood and tossed their half-finished drinks before heading for the exit himself. “Have a good day, Willa.”

“You too,” I called, though he was already gone, leaving me staring around the empty bookstore and wondering if it was something I said. Pandora stretched on the cushion beside me, and I reached over to pat her head while I drank my coffee and ruminated. “Seems the Mystic Notch grapevine isn’t helping shed any light on Albert’s death, is it, girl?” I scratched Pandora behind her ears and laughed when she all but melted against my hand. “Too bad I don’t have my globe here with me to conjure Albert’s ghost. I bet he could answer my questions once and for all.”

* * *

Pandora squinted up at Willa and managed not to roll her eyes, barely. If her human would just drink the dandelion tea like she’d wanted her to, then she could see old Albert’s ghost just fine, globe or not.

She stretched out on the sofa and stared up at the ceiling of the bookstore, Albert's ghost floating as plain as day above them. He looked nearly as anxious as Pandora felt. Her idea had fizzled out last night. Sure, her antics on the counter had gotten Willa to think about drinking the tea, but with the arrival of Striker, Willa had forgotten all about the mug and left it half-full on the coffee table. She'd only caught a glimpse of Albert, and then "poof," he'd vanished when Striker had arrived.

It was all so frustrating, trying to get these inferior humans to communicate properly with their feline companions as any civilized being should. In one last effort, Pandora jumped down and padded over to the counter, where she jumped up and managed to snag one of the tea bags out of Willa's purse. She carried it back to the sofa and plopped it down onto Willa's lap in the most blatant way she could think of. Did it work? No. Willa just sat there, sipping that icky coffee and staring at nothing.

Why couldn't she have belonged to a human like Bing? Now that man knew how to communicate. He'd even sent Pandora several encouraging messages telepathically before he'd left the shop. If it hadn't been for that brief spot of enlightenment, Pandora might've given up on the whole venture.

Even Pepper knew how to communicate with a cat, though her communication was mostly one-way. She didn't receive Pandora's responses but still somehow knew that Pandora could understand her. Pepper was more enlightened about magic. She even infused it into her teas. Okay, well, Pandora had to admit sometimes that didn't always work out as Pepper planned. Hopefully, that wouldn't be the case with the dandelion tea. Pandora really needed it to work to help Willa see Albert. Her status with the cats of Mystic Notch depended on it, not to mention the entire future of the town.

She reached over and batted the tea bag in Willa's lap with her paw once more, and this time her human finally noticed it.

"Did you bring me this, sweetie?" Willa held up the tea bag by its string. "You know, I think I will have some tea. It might help my leg feel better."

She got up and limped away. Pandora said a silent prayer of thanks to the cat god Bastet that her human had finally gotten the message. Now, if she'd just get on board with other things, they'd be all set. Like the glass globe in her living room. And Striker.

In truth, Pandora wanted nothing more than to get those two together. Striker was a good human. He'd saved Pandora once, and he was a good match for Willa. Plus, she'd sensed he was far more open to cross-species communication than he'd let on. Pandora knew Striker could see ghosts too. Just like Willa. She'd discovered that little tidbit several months ago when she'd helped him solve a murder. She'd also discovered that he was as desperate to hide it from Willa as Willa was to hide it from him.

Pandora would never understand why Willa and Striker felt the need to hide the fact that they saw the dead. In the feline world, being able to see ghosts like Pandora could was a rare and coveted skill. But then many things humans did didn't make sense to her.

It was kind of comical, though, watching them try to hide their spiritual skills from each other. Pandora had witnessed it herself a few months ago, and it cracked her up the way both Willa and Striker would get all nervous whenever a ghost appeared to them while they were in each other's presence. They would stammer and shift and turn about, trying to "hide" the ghost from the other. It was all for nothing because, while both Willa and Striker could see ghosts, they could not see the same *ghosts.*

Was there something she could do about this? If only Willa and Striker could confide their ghostly sightings to each other, she knew it would make their relationship stronger. And the only way they could prove it to each other was to have them see the same ghost at the same time.

She glanced over at Willa making her tea at the counter. Maybe she could get both humans to drink the tea at the same time and see the same ghost. Albert's ghost. That would certainly bring them together, right?

Willa carried her mug back over to the sofa and settled into her seat once more, sipping the tea slowly. Soon, she was staring wide-eyed up at the ceiling, where Albert floated overhead, and Pandora smiled inwardly. About time. She curled up in a corner of the sofa for a much-needed catnap, dreaming of ways to set her new plan to bring Willa and Striker together into action.

I STARED up into Albert's ghostly face, shocked. The fact he was here, now, meant that he'd been murdered. Robert and Franklin had been right the previous day. Poor Albert did look confused, his shyness apparent in the way he kept disappearing and reappearing at regular intervals.

I was finally seeing Albert. Hopefully, no customers would come in. Not that I didn't want customers, just not right now.

"Hello, Albert," I said, plastering on what I hoped was a reassuring smile. "I'm so glad you finally decided to visit me. What is it you want my help with?"

Several seconds passed in silence until finally

Albert said, "The letter. I need to make sure it gets delivered."

"Okay," I said, my heart rate speeding. So there had been a letter, and most likely, it was the reason Albert had been killed. "Can you tell me about what happened at the post office, Albert? Who was there with you? Who took the letter from you?"

Albert's form wavered on the ceiling, and he opened his mouth as if to answer. Then the bells on the front door jangled, and he disappeared in a *POOF!*

Disappointment zinged through me as I looked over to see Striker walk in. Twice now, he'd interrupted my time with Albert, and I was starting to take it personally, no matter how cute Striker was. I got up and walked over to set my mug on the counter then grab the stack of books that needed to be reshelved. I shot Striker a small smile as I passed him. "Good morning. To what do I owe this honor?"

"I just finished talking to Gus and thought I'd stop by." He leaned a hip against the counter, all masculine grace and confidence. "Figured you might want to know, since you were so curious last night."

His new information on the murder helped ease my irritation with him considerably. I kept working while he talked, not wanting to seem too eager. "Sure. What did you discover?"

"Well, turns out Albert Schumer was murdered. That's why Gus called me in. It was obvious by the way the body was positioned. He'd been pushed then hit on the back of the head. Whoever killed him tried to make it look like Albert had slipped and fallen, bashing his head on the steps, but Gus found the rock they used in the shrubs nearby."

"That's awful." I peeked around the end of a bookcase to see him. "Any fingerprints?"

"Nope." His gray gaze narrowed, and his frowned deepened. "Mind telling me why you were so curious last night, Willa? If you know something about what happened to Albert, it would be best for you to tell me now."

"No." I scowled, glancing up at the ceiling again before I could stop myself, but thankfully, there was no sign of his ghost. "How would I know anything about what happened to that poor man?"

"I don't know. That's why I'm asking," Striker said, following me between the shelves. "You seem to have a knack for trouble where these cases are concerned, Chance."

"Well, I don't know anything," I said dismissively, hoping to put some space between us and this awkward conversation. It wasn't like I could tell him the truth about me seeing ghosts. That would get me a nice long trip to the state mental hospital. And I didn't want to lie to Striker, not when we were just starting to explore this connection and attraction between us. That seemed wrong on way too many levels. So I kept my head down and my hands busy with work. "I was just making small talk."

Meow!

Pandora ran between us, dodging left and then leaping right. What was with her? I didn't remember leaving any catnip out, but she sure was acting crazed.

"Small talk, huh?" Striker snorted, trailing behind me down the narrow space between the shelves.

"Yep." I placed a pristine hard copy of one of my favorite Nancy Drew mysteries, *The Secret of the Old Clock*, face out on the shelf in the mystery aisle and headed over toward the reference section.

Meroop!

Pandora raced in front of Striker. He sidestepped quickly to avoid her then tripped over the bookshelf and smacked his knee hard on the edge of the solid metal bookshelf on the opposite side of the aisle. With a muttered curse, he straightened and rubbed what had to be a sore spot. "Talking about dead people is small talk to you?"

Yes. "No." I turned to face him at last. "Look, I'm sorry I brought up Albert Schumer, okay? It was an innocent mistake. I swear. Won't happen again. You want some ice for your knee? I can grab some from the freezer in the break room."

"No, I'm fine." He sighed and rubbed a hand over his face. "I need to get back to work." He stepped toward me, narrowly missing Pandora, who darted behind him on the way to her plush cat bed in the front window, her kinked tail high in the air. "I think Pandora has been cooped up too long. She's acting crazy."

"Hopefully, she'll sleep it off."

Striker dropped a kiss on top of my head. "Stay safe, and please don't poke around in the mess with Albert. We don't even know what we're dealing with here yet. Okay?"

"Okay," I said, knowing it wasn't true. Albert Schumer had sought me out, asked for my help. It was my duty to assist him with this last task so that he could rest in peace for eternity. If I didn't, who knew what else could happen?

7

"Are you sure this is a good idea?" Pepper asked me later as we drove to Albert Schumer's house.

Well, actually, no. I wasn't sure it was such a great idea, but I couldn't think of anything else to do. I'd concentrated, tried to distract myself with work, even meditated during my lunch hour—not to mention I chugged enough dandelion tea that day to float a cruise ship—but Albert's ghost had never reappeared. After what Striker had told me, I had to find out more about that missing letter. Since Grace Schumer had mentioned the letter to Elspeth, it was possible she might have more information.

Pepper, of course, was like the town's grief counselor, personally visiting each deceased person's family and bringing them her healing herbal tea. She'd been doing it for years, even before I'd left for college, so it kind of gave us the perfect excuse to go to the Schumer house today, even if my best friend was uncomfortable with my ulterior motives.

"I wonder if Gemma will be there," Pepper said as we turned onto the side street where Albert had lived.

"Who's Gemma?"

"Albert's daughter. She's married to Desmond Lacroix."

At her disapproving tone, I glanced over to see her pursed lips. "I take it you don't care for this person?"

"No, I don't." Which was rare where Pepper was concerned. She liked everybody. "Desmond is one of those people who is always trying to get out of their responsibilities. He's always trying to weasel out of an honest day's work."

"Hmm." I pulled up to the curb in front of the Schumer household and cut the engine. "Sounds like a real prize."

"Yes, I'm not sure what Gemma sees in him." Pepper exited the passenger side of my vehicle. I got out and locked up then followed her up to the front door. Grace Schumer answered after one knock, looking understandably sad and tearful. Pepper immediately pulled her into a soothing hug while I stood awkwardly behind them, holding Pepper's tea cozy for her.

Grace pulled away at last and welcomed us into her home, sniffling as she closed the door. "The police were just here. They informed us that Albert's death was a murder. Who would do such a thing?"

I handed the tea cozy back to Pepper as Gemma rushed forward to comfort her mother, who was sobbing again. Leaning against the wall of the small living room was who I assumed to be Desmond, looking bored with everything. His expression hovered somewhere between anger and guilt, and his hand was bandaged. My mind, of course, went into overdrive.

Based on what Pepper had told me about him on the way over, it was entirely possible he'd had something to do with Albert's death. Perhaps he'd thought he'd inherit money or something, though that really didn't make any sense now that I thought about it. With both Grace and Gemma alive, any inheritance would go to them first. But if Gemma got money, Desmond would benefit, plus I didn't like Desmond's attitude. I made a beeline over to him to size him up for myself.

"I'm Willa Chance. I own the local bookstore." I

held out my hand for him to shake, knowing full well he'd have a hard time doing it with his injury.

He held up his bandaged hand and shrugged. "Desmond Lacroix. Son-in-law."

"How'd you hurt your hand?" I asked, not feeling the least bit bad about my nosiness.

"Carpal tunnel. Just had another surgery to try and fix it." He shifted his attention to Pepper, who'd just joined us. "Oh, you brought your healing tea," Desmond said sarcastically, ignoring Pepper's glare of distaste. "That should do the trick and fix me right up."

To head off what I sensed would be a stern dressing down from my best friend of the man beside me, I herded Pepper toward the coffee table and helped her set up her tea service. When she was done, she took a seat beside Grace, handing her a cup of tea.

"This tea should help soothe you." Pepper patted Grace's hand. "I do hope you'll let me know if you need more."

"Thank you, dear." Grace sipped her tea. "This is all so disturbing."

"I can imagine," I said. "I mean it's one thing to be left without a husband and with the financial burden of a funeral and burial and all, but then to discover it was murder..." I shook my head sympathetically and avoided Pepper's narrow-eyed glare. I knew my mention of finances hadn't been very subtle, and Pepper wouldn't like me interrogating the widow. But money was one of the primary motives for murder, and I needed to know if anyone would benefit from Albert's death financially.

Grace dabbed at her eyes with a tissue. "Thankfully, I won't have to worry about finances. Albert had great life insurance from the post office and a nice pension too."

"Well, at least that's something." I grabbed a scone off the china dish and bit in. It was almond flavored with thin slices of almonds.

"I still can't imagine who would want my Albert dead," Grace said. "He was such a sweet, helpful, kind man. It must have been a random killing."

Desmond gave a derisive snort. "Or he made someone angry."

"What do you mean?" I asked.

Desmond's eyes narrowed, and he shifted position. "Albert was always fighting with Barney Delaney. I saw them myself just the other day, yelling at each other right there on Main Street in front of everyone. If you ask me, Barney's the one the police should be looking at. If I had to guess, I'd say Barney got sick of arguing with my father-in-law and decided to put a stop to it for good."

8

After leaving the Schumer home and dropping Pepper off at her tea shop, I headed back to Last Chance Books. I parked my truck in its usual spot in the narrow alleyway beside the building then went inside to check that things were running smoothly.

Hanna, the assistant I'd hired, was busy helping customers at the counter, and everything else looked to be in order. I checked the mail and dropped off my purse in the office then headed back out to follow up on what Desmond had told me about the feud between his father-in-law and Barney Delaney. It was a thin lead at best. No one murdered someone just because they argued a lot, did they?

Hmm... hadn't Cordelia said that Barney always lost to Albert in checkers? Was that what they argued about? Who would murder someone just to win in checkers? As far as I knew, the contest didn't have any prize other than boasting rights, and they'd been playing against each other for years. Why kill him now?

Delaney's Antique Emporium was down two blocks and around the corner from my bookstore. The afternoon air was crisp and cool, and weak sunshine filtered through the puffy, gray clouds above. Barney Delaney was in his late seventies and had owned the antique store for more than twenty years, ever since he'd retired from being the town's postmaster and way before I returned to town.

Inside the shop, it was like entering a different world. Soothing instrumental music played from the overhead speakers. The air smelled of exotic spices and old memories. In the main part of the store, antique furniture was set up to mimic different rooms, as it would be in a house. Stained-glass lamps sat on oak side tables next to blue brocade sofas with carved mahogany backs.

Beyond that, the store was divided into sections for various items—furniture, rugs, artwork, ceramics, kitchenware, books, and periodicals. There was even an extensive grouping of old post office memorabilia and another for rare stamps and coins.

I spotted Barney behind the counter near the register and made my way over to him, passing a lovely old checkers set made from expensive ebony, ivory, and marble. Barney watched me with a wary gaze, and I did my best to put him at ease.

"Your shop looks as beautiful as always," I said, hoping to win some points with him.

"Thanks," he said, turning away, a frown etching his weathered face. So much for making a good impression. He wasn't exactly known as the most talkative guy around town, or the friendliest. Barney Delaney kept mostly to himself, except for the yearly checkers tournament. And fighting with Albert Schumer, apparently. "What can I help you with today, Miss Chance?"

"Oh, please. Call me Willa." My smile faltered slightly when he just stared at me. "Um, I wondered if I might ask you a few questions."

"Depends."

"On what?"

"On what they're about," he said, his bushy white eyebrows knitting together. "I've got a shop to run here. Best make it fast."

"Right." I glanced around the empty store then back to him, forcing my smile wider. "I just left the Schumer household. Terrible thing that happened to poor Albert, huh?" I glanced up to see his reaction, but Barney was busy sorting through receipts on the counter, his expression unreadable. "Anyway, Albert's son-in-law, Desmond, mentioned you'd had a fight with Albert shortly before he died. I wondered if you might tell me what that argument was about."

Barney gave me a long flat look over the tops of his wire-rim glasses, his gaze narrowed. "There was no argument."

"But Desmond said he clearly saw you and Albert—"

"We were having a lively discussion," Barney continued, talking over me. "Albert was my friend. That's just how we communicated."

"Hmm." I glanced over at the expensive checkers set again, searching for common ground. "You must be looking forward to this year's tournament. Rumor has it you're a shoo-in to win, with Albert gone."

Barney froze, his fists clenching on the wooden countertop, the sound of crinkling paper filling the air as he crushed the receipts in his hands. "What exactly are you implying, Miss Chance?"

Heat prickled my cheeks as I realized I'd put my foot in it this time. "Oh, uh, nothing. I was just talking to Cordelia Deering this morning—she and her sister,

Hattie, are regulars at my shop each day, you know—and she mentioned your skill with the game and—"

"I had nothing to do with Albert Schumer's death," Barney said, coming around the end of the counter to stand before me. Even for an elderly guy, he was still a good foot taller than I, and in relatively good shape, lean and sinewy. If the hard glint in his icy-blue eyes was any indication, he was furious. Perhaps the argument Desmond claimed he saw had merit after all. Tension pulsed off Barney in waves, and I could well imagine him fighting with poor Albert then whacking him on the head hard enough to kill him. I could also imagine him doing the same to me. "Like I said, Albert was my friend. And why would I murder someone to win that checkers tournament? There isn't even a cash prize."

"I never meant to imply anything, Mr. Delaney," I said, inching away from him slowly and moving nearer to the door. "Honestly. Like I said, Desmond had these concerns, and I promised I'd ask about them the next time I saw you." I gave a nervous laugh. "My past as a crime reporter's to blame. I'm too curious and nosy. At least that's what Striker always tells me." I figured it didn't hurt to name-drop my law enforcement boyfriend to give Barney second thoughts about clonking me on the head and pushing me out onto the steps.

He took a deep breath and exhaled slowly, his shoulders slumping slightly and his head lowering. The corners of his mouth turned down, and I caught a glimpse of a man who'd just lost an old, and possibly only, friend. Sympathy bubbled up inside me before I tamped it down.

"Look, I'm sorry I jumped all over you there, Miss Chance. I guess this whole thing with Albert's just thrown me for a loop." He moved back behind the register again, his anger apparently mollified and his tone contrite. "But I'll tell you something. If you're looking for suspects in Albert's death, I'd look no further than his own family. That no-good son-in-law of his was leeching off Albert. Last I heard, Desmond had gotten into some shady deal with Nathan Anderson involving Albert's old stamp collection." Barney shook his head. "In fact, Desmond came in here earlier this morning with a bunch of stamps he found in Albert's old things from the post office. The man's not even in his grave yet, and that schmuck's trying to profit off him."

My mind spun with the new information. Desmond must have been in town just before Pepper and I showed up at the Schumer house then. I wondered if Gemma had any idea what her husband was up to. Then I wondered if any of those stamps had come from the missing letter from the murder scene. "Can I see what he brought in?"

"No, you can't." Barney scowled. "I didn't buy them. Flat-out refused. I told him I wanted nothing to do with his schemes and blood money. Desmond was as mad as a hatter about it, but I didn't care."

9

I left Barney's shop shortly thereafter, my thoughts racing. Because of the nice weather, I decided to walk the long way back to the store. I'd be sitting most of the afternoon and cataloguing new books into my software system once Hanna went home, so the exercise would do me good.

So, Desmond had tried to sell Barney stamps from Albert's collection before they'd even had the funeral. Then he'd turned around and tried to implicate Barney. And now Nathan Anderson was involved in some deal gone bad with Desmond too. I didn't know much about Nathan, except he was involved with Felicity Bates—a woman of wealth and means and mystery who lived in a huge mansion on the outskirts of Mystic Notch. She'd inherited her wealth from her husband, who'd died a while back, and the mansion was actually his family home. Felicity lived there with her son and in-laws.

I wasn't exactly sure what Felicity did all day. She didn't work. That was for sure. I knew she fancied herself to be a witch and usually made an appearance when there was anything reputed to be magical around. She'd been after that recipe book that Elspeth now had and an old vial of some goop that Hester Warren had buried on her property three hundred years ago. Not that I believed in magic, but Felicity apparently did. I wasn't particularly fond of Felicity or her cat, a long-haired white feline named Fluff who seemed to rub my Pandora the wrong way.

I'd had several run-ins with Felicity and her cat after my return to Mystic Notch, and frankly, I wouldn't put murder past that woman. After all, one of her kids was in jail for the same crime. Maybe it was genetic.

As I rounded the corner, I spotted my sister, Gus, standing outside the bookstore. I made a beeline for her, hoping maybe she had some new information on Albert's case. But as I got closer, I could tell by the look on her face that she was not pleased. Not good. Not good at all.

"Hey," I said as I drew up beside Gus. "What's going on?"

"Why don't you tell me?" Gus said, removing all doubt about her temper. She would have been more formidable if she didn't look like a Barbie in sheriff's garb with her hourglass figure and delicate features. Even pulling her long blond hair back into a severe ponytail didn't do much to make her look fierce. The gun at her hip and her dour expression did, though. "Are you sticking your nose into my investigation after I expressly told you not to, Willa?"

While Gus went off, reading me the usual riot act about danger and being a civilian, I glanced inside the shop. Pandora was perched on the back of the purple sofa, staring at me with those emerald eyes of hers, and I'd swear I saw a smirk on her little feline face. I wasn't sure cats could smirk, but if they could, my cat was definitely doing it.

Gus was still going strong, and I crossed my arms. "I'm not butting into your investigation."

"Yeah?" My sister stepped closer, her expression unconvinced. "And where were you just now?"

"At the antique store."

"Barney Delaney's place?"

"Unless there's another one in town I don't know about, yes." My toe tapped incessantly against the sidewalk, a small concession to the irritation growing inside me. I was a grown woman. A business owner. I did not need to stand here and be lectured to by my sister, sheriff or not. "Why?"

"Why did you go over there?"

"Well, I..." Darn. I tried to come up with some plausible excuse for leaving the bookstore in the middle of the day to go antique shopping but came up empty. Didn't matter anyway. Gus wasn't buying my excuse. She never did. "Fine. I went to talk to him about Albert. But I'm not poking into your case. I swear."

"You better not, Willa." Gus clenched her jaw. "I'm telling you to stay out of official police business. Leave it to the trained professionals who know how to work a case. I've got it covered." With that, she turned on her heel and headed back toward her squad car parked at the curb. I waited until she'd pulled away before I went inside.

Hanna finished up her shift then left for the day. I took a seat behind the counter and gave Pandora a skeptical look. She purred loudly and went back to sleep. Things were slow around the shop, so I reshelved for a while then opened a few boxes of new stock we'd received and set about making a new display. Out of the blue, Pandora sat up and hissed.

"What's the matter, girl?" I asked, glancing out the front windows of the shop. The window looked out on Main Street, running from two feet off the floor to the ten-foot-high ceiling. Standing on the sidewalk right outside was none other than Felicity Bates, and she was arguing with... Nathan Anderson! Speak of the devils.

Whatever they were fighting about, they both looked heated—their hands flying and their faces flushed. I sidled closer, hoping to perhaps overhear some of their conversation without being too obvious about my snooping. Unfortunately, the big plate-glass windows really did dampen the sound. I scooched over to the edge of the window, leaning closer. I couldn't hear a thing except the odd snatch of words—something about a note or letter and stamps. My eyes widened, and my pulse sped. Could they be arguing about Albert's missing letter?

I was trying to work out how Felicity's interest in magic might translate into stamps and letters when Fluff leapt up on his hind legs, his face smashing into the window right in front of Pandora. He hissed nastily, his leash dangling from the matching pink collar around his neck. I supposed I would've been upset too if I were a male cat, made to wear a ridiculous fuchsia-and-rhinestone monstrosity like that.

Pandora was caught off guard and tumbled off the windowsill to the floor, poor thing. At the sound of the cat hissing, Felicity and Nathan both turned to stare at Fluff then through the windows into the shop at me. I jumped back, praying they hadn't seen me spying on them.

10

Pandora scrambled to her feet then shook her head and stuck her tail up as if she'd meant to do that all along. How dare Fluff awaken her so rudely? Damn that cat, always causing trouble. She peeked up over the windowsill to see Fluff standing outside, laughing evilly as he licked his paw and stared back at her.

"I see your human is still leading you around," Pandora said, hoping to get a reaction out of him. She leapt up onto the sixteen-inch-wide ledge at the bottom of the window where her cat bed sat and settled on her haunches, giving her a height advantage as she glared out the window at the other cat.

Fluff stopped his grooming long enough to meet her gaze levelly. "No one leads me anywhere I don't want to go. We both know I'm in charge."

"Maybe," Pandora said, giving a small shrug. "But what brings you here? Is it this letter your humans are arguing about?"

That woman Felicity wasn't to be trusted. All the cats knew her and were wary of her powers. She was a dark one, with minor natural talents she sought to improve. And she was just the type to want to dig up all the ingredients for the pleasantry charm that Hester Warren had buried. She'd like nothing better than to be able to swoop in and grow her evil powers if the spell should become reversed.

The man with Felicity, Nathan Anderson, Pandora wasn't as familiar with. She had thought he was a friend of the local feral cats, but if he was hanging around with Felicity Bates, then she might have to reconsider that opinion. After all, it wouldn't be the first time things weren't as they seemed in Mystic Notch.

Fluff, of course, continued to play dumb. "Letter? I don't know anything about a letter."

"Sure you don't." Pandora stretched then lifted a paw to preen. "I think perhaps all those rhinestones are starting to affect your brain."

"You're just jealous because your poor human will never be able to buy you such fine things to wear." Fluff raised his chin haughtily. The effect, however, was ruined when Felicity tugged on the leash attached to his harness and yanked the cat backward, causing him to stumble over

his own paws. He glared into the shop, first at Pandora then at Willa, who was hiding off to the side. If she lived through all nine lives and beyond, Pandora would never understand all these silly humans acting ridiculous. A cat would strut proudly, not hide away in the shadows.

Pandora yawned, watching as Felicity led Fluff away. Nathan took off in the opposite direction, his steps hard and his expression harder. She'd file that information away to think about and analyze later. Perhaps there was something to be learned that would help her cause. The cats of Mystic Notch would be interested to know that Felicity might be seeking the letter. For now, it was time for another catnap. A girl needed her beauty sleep after all, and her last nap had been so rudely interrupted.

11

Striker came over for dinner again that night. Honestly, I was starting to wonder if seeing him so often was a good thing. Not that I didn't enjoy his company. I did, perhaps too much. See, up until the last couple of months, we'd been pretty much on-again, off-again. Now, we were in an "on" phase—very much "on." And don't get me wrong, I liked Striker. A lot.

But there was a big secret I was keeping from him—namely the fact I could see and communicate with ghosts. To most men, that would be a deal breaker, so I hadn't told him. Hadn't told anyone except Pepper. Once I did come out with the truth, things with Striker would be over. I was sure. I guess I just wanted our little bit of normal to last a tad longer.

He texted me to let me know he was bringing pizza, and I sent back a thumbs-up emoji. Good thing because all I had in the fridge was cottage cheese and whipped cream in the can. For such a small town, Mystic Notch had some great eateries, and Debrazzi's pizza was one of my faves. I set out plates and napkins on the kitchen table then settled into a corner of the sofa to wait. Honestly, before Striker had offered to come over, I'd planned on spending my night with a fresh pot of dandelion tea and Albert's ghost. After speaking with the Schumer family and, later, Barney, I really wanted to get more information directly from the source.

Seeing as my fridge was empty and my stomach was growling, however, I changed my mind. Besides, I could always hold a powwow with Albert after Striker left. *If* Albert would appear. If he didn't, I guessed I was on my own.

I was scrolling through my emails when a loud, outraged hiss emanated from the porch, followed by a muttered, masculine curse and a dull thud. I rushed over to the door and opened it to find Pandora scampering to the far end of the wooden porch while Striker pulled himself up from the floor, the pizza box precariously balanced on one hand. I took the food from him and held the door until he was inside. He was limping slightly, and I frowned. "What happened?"

"Your cat tripped me. That's what happened." He hobbled over to the table and plopped down, rubbing his sore knee. Pandora squeezed through the crack in the door before I closed it, giving me an innocent look as she passed. I knew better.

"I'm so sorry." I took the pizza into the kitchen. "Is that the same knee you banged earlier?"

"Yeah, hurts like heck."

"You're in luck. Pepper gave me some tea earlier that's supposed to help with joint pain. My leg was killing me this morning, and I will say it did help. Should get your knee back to normal in no time."

"I don't know, Chance," Striker said, grimacing. "I'm not much of an herbal tea guy."

"Trust me, you'll like this. It's made from dandelions. Go lounge on the sofa, and I'll bring this stuff in."

Striker did as told, and I filled my kettle with water, set it on high, then brought the pizza back into the living room along with the plates and napkins I'd put out earlier. I set it all on the coffee table before us. I figured we could eat here and be cozy, and I could save Striker the pain of moving around until his knee felt better. "So, how was your day? Any big doings in Dixford Pass?"

"Nah. Couple of missing chickens I tracked down this afternoon. And a loitering charge filed against a college kid who'd gotten a little too besotted with his sweetheart and was hanging around her front yard too much. The dad wanted to teach him a lesson, so I got called in. No harm done." He cracked open the pizza box, and the succulent aromas of melted cheese and rich tomato sauce filled the air. He'd gotten pepperoni and mushroom, my favorite. After serving us each up a slice, Striker closed the box and sat back to eat.

I did my best to ignore the enticing way his navy-blue T-shirt stretched over his muscled chest and arms or how the deep-blue color brought out the stormy gray of his eyes.

"How about you, Chance. Hear any more about Albert?"

I opened my mouth to answer but was halted by the screech of the kettle in the kitchen. Talk about saved by the bell. I excused myself and hurried off to fix us each a mug of tea. Knowing its effect on me, I didn't want to drink too much in front of Striker for fear I'd start seeing my undead friend again. He bravely tried his, declared it "not so bad after all," and promptly downed half a cup. I refilled it for him then settled in to eat.

"I haven't heard anything new, really, about Albert's case," I said around a bite of food. It wasn't completely the truth, what with the conversations I'd had, but I didn't want to say too much because Gus had told me to stay out of it and I knew that my sister and Striker talked on a professional basis. "Pepper and I did go see the Schumer family this morning, to pay our respects."

"Hmm." Striker gave me a narrowed glance. "I hope for your sake that's all it was, Chance. I don't like you putting yourself in danger in a murder investigation."

I nodded and sipped more of my tea, noticing Pandora sitting on the armchair across from me. She was staring at the crystal globe paperweight on the table as if hypnotized. I looked too and spotted strange, muted colors reflecting in the glass. If I squinted, it almost looked like there was some kind of letter trapped inside, the writing faded and looping. I set my mug of tea aside and leaned forward for a closer inspection, but as I did so, wisps of smoke began to gather in the corner opposite me.

Oh no. Albert!

My eyes widened, and I bit my lips. It wasn't like I

could just tell him to come back at a more convenient time. I tried jerking my head in a not-so-subtle gesture for him to beat it, but no such luck.

"Everything okay, Willa?" Striker asked, watching me with a concerned expression. His gaze darted from me to the corner where my attention was focused, and he got a funny look on his face. Probably realizing what a weirdo he was dating. "Uh, hey, is that a band of turkeys out there?"

"What? Where?" I looked out the window where Striker was pointing but didn't see any turkeys.

"Forget about the turkeys, and listen to me. My death was no accident." Albert's ghost swirled up in front of us, blocking the window. Great, *now* he wanted to tell me all about his death. Perfect. Too bad I couldn't ask him how he knew that and who was behind it with Striker in here. I made a face at Albert, hoping he'd get the message, but when Striker turned in my direction, I plastered on an innocent look.

"Oh wait, is that a deer?" I pointed out the other window, hoping to distract Striker long enough to make some get-lost gesture that Albert would understand.

"I don't see anything..."

Albert swirled in front of us again. "What is wrong with you people? I need your help."

Striker took my hand and pulled me up from the couch. "On second thought, that might be a deer. A whole herd of them. Let's go out and see."

I seized the opportunity, scrambling to my feet. "Yes. Fresh air would do us both good, I think."

Luckily, it was unseasonably warm that night, since neither of us seemed particularly worried about coats.

"Uh, yeah. Fresh air," he mumbled, distracted. Striker opened the door and all but shoved me out onto the porch then stumbled outside with me. "I, um, thought I saw a moose at the edge of your property when I pulled up," he said, his voice quiet and distant.

What was wrong with him? He was acting odd... Shoot! This was it. He'd realized I was too strange for him and was breaking it off. Oh well, it was fun while it lasted.

We both turned to gaze out at the darkening tree line of my property. A warm breeze scented with decaying leaves and dirt stirred. I remained silent while I waited for him to drop the bomb. After a while, when he didn't say anything, my pulse began to slow and my tense shoulders relaxed as the warm breeze drifted past us. Maybe he couldn't figure out how to word it. Knowing Striker and the nice guy that he was,

I thought he was probably trying to figure out how to break it to me gently.

Maybe I should help him out. But I didn't have time to think about how to do that because just then, Albert's ghostly form materialized through the wall of the house to stand near us on the porch and I nearly gagged on my tongue. Albert gave me a peevish stare and said, "If anyone cares, I was shoved."

Striker grabbed my shoulders and turned me away from Albert. *Here it comes, the big breakup.*

Albert glided over beside Striker, and Striker turned me in the other direction. "The moose was right over there."

"Oh." I looked in the direction Striker was pointing. Maybe he wasn't breaking up with me.

We only had a few seconds of peace, staring off into the woods, before Albert swirled before us again. I grabbed Striker's hand. "Maybe we should go back inside."

Striker was staring at the woods still, right through Albert's ghost. His face was pale, his jaw tight. "Yeah, we should go somewhere..."

"Listen! I've had enough," Albert yelled in his spooky spirit voice, somewhere between a deep, bellowing gust and a foghorn. "You *both* need to stop and listen to me! Right now!"

Even Striker seemed taken aback at Albert's loud proclamation. Wait a minute... Striker... taken aback? But how could that be? And then I realized what Albert had just said.

"Both?" Striker and I said the word at the same time.

Albert nodded. "Both."

Striker slowly met my gaze, his eyes filled with wariness and wonder. "Both."

12

"Wait a minute..." I started.

"You can see..." Striker said at the same time.

"Yes, yes." Albert gave a dismissive wave of his misty hand. "You both can see me, right?"

Heart clogging my throat, I gave a slow nod. Striker did the same. All at once, I didn't feel so alone anymore. Pandora meowed triumphantly from the window, where she had been watching us from inside. If Striker could see Albert, see ghosts like I could, then maybe he wouldn't think I was too weird for him after all. Maybe this could develop into something more between us. Maybe... I still had to be sure, had to hear the words.

"So, you can see Albert, right now?" I asked.

"Yes." Some of the color had returned to Striker's cheeks, though he still looked as gobsmacked as I felt. "And you can too?"

"I believed we've cleared this up," Albert said, his tone growing impatient again. "Now, if you'll both pay attention, I have something important to—"

"How long have you been able to see ghosts?" I continued as if Albert hadn't spoken.

"For as long as I can remember. When I was a kid, it used to scare me senseless. As I got older, I tried to ignore it, hoping it would go away one day. It never did." Striker exhaled slowly, leaning his hand on the porch banister for support. "And you?"

"Just since my car accident. When I came to afterward, I could see the spirits. At first, I thought I'd gone crazy, but now I'm sort of used to it. No one knows about this except Pepper, though." I bit my lip, frowning down at my toes. "Well, and now you."

"Same here. I mean, I haven't told anyone about this curse except you. And my parents knew, but they're both gone now."

"Hello!" Albert's voice boomed once more, and both Striker and I winced. "Important information here. Someone was after that envelope I was intending to mail. I found it in an old mailbag at home while I was cleaning out my stuff. I might be retired, but it's still my sworn duty to make sure every letter gets processed."

"Who was the letter addressed to, Albert?" I asked.

"It was from Helen Warren to a woman named Dorothy Hill."

"Huh." Striker scratched his chin and frowned. "Helen Warren, I've heard of but not this Dorothy Hill. And that letter had to have been decades old. Why would anyone kill for that?" He shook his head. "Was the stamp valuable?"

"Not that I know of." Albert attempted to sit on one of the rockers but simply floated through it.

I leaned my hips against the railing, struggling to take in everything I'd just learned. Striker could see ghosts, the same as me. Except he'd apparently been born with the talent—if that was what you wanted to call it—while mine had only happened after my accident. Of course, I didn't mention the rest of the weird stuff that had come along with my surprise gift and my return to Mystic Notch. Things like that old recipe book that Pepper had said was really filled with old spells. Or the fact I thought I'd seen Evie turn a person into a toad (I was still unclear on that one, though. The EMT had said the smoke inhalation might have messed with my perception of what happened, but it seemed so real). Or the message I'd received from

Adelaide Hamilton's ghost this past summer that had supposedly been from my grandmother telling me to believe in magic. The whole I-see-dead-people thing was bad enough. I didn't want Striker to think I was beyond crazy.

"Hey," Striker said, moving closer to me in the twilight. He tipped my chin up with his finger and smiled that sexy little smile of his, the one that always made my toes curl and my knees wobble. "I like that we have this new connection, this secret bond about the ghosts." His thumb stroked my cheek softly, and I gripped the railing tighter to keep from melting into a puddle of goo at his feet. "You know, when I was growing up, my grandma always told me about these magical gifts that were passed down in my family, and she said I was special. For the first time in my life, I'm actually glad I'm different. Because you're different too, Willa. You're truly special."

My lips tingled, and my breath hitched, my eyes drifting closed as he lowered his head to kiss me. I clutched my fingers into the front of his soft blue T-shirt, rising up on tiptoe to meet him and...

"Right," Albert said, clearing his throat loudly. Striker and I flew apart like opposing magnets. "Well, this is nice and all, but before you two get all lovey-dovey, you should know that the killer wanted that letter badly enough to murder me for it. Now, go and find him."

Albert disappeared in a puff of smoke, leaving Striker and me to stare at each other in the gathering darkness. Our breaths rasped loudly, and the air suddenly turned chilly. I let us back inside and took a seat on the sofa, staring once more at the paperweight on the coffee table.

"Before Albert showed up, I thought I saw a letter reflected inside that globe." I pointed to the paperweight, and Striker picked it up, holding it in his palm. I leaned over to peer inside the glass again, but all I could see was the reflection of Striker's hand. He had some scratches I hadn't noticed. "It's gone now."

He set it back on the table, and I glanced at his hand, wondering what had scratched him. No scratches.

Weird.

Probably just an odd reflection of light from the paperweight.

"So, what's our next move?" Striker asked, settling back against the cushions and stretching his arm along the back of the sofa. I battled the insane urge to cuddle into his side and instead pushed myself farther back into the corner of my seat. We had work to do.

"Well, when Pepper and I went to see the

Schumers today, I got to meet Desmond, Albert's son-in-law. I also got an earful about him from Pepper, about how Desmond doesn't like to work and is always trying out some money-making scheme." I crossed my arms and frowned. "I went to see Barney Delaney afterward. He said that Desmond was in his shop right after Albert died, attempting to pawn off Albert's rare stamp collection. Do you think he might've stolen the letter, thinking it was valuable due to its age?"

"Could be," Striker said, his expression thoughtful as he picked up a slice of pizza.

"Oh, and did I mention that after I got back to my shop, I overheard Nathan Anderson and Felicity Bates arguing on the sidewalk? It was about a letter too."

"Felicity Bates, eh?" Striker chewed on his slice. "This wouldn't be the first time she was a suspect in a murder investigation. Her family isn't exactly the most upstanding in the community, despite all their money. After all, Felicity's son is in jail for murder right now. Let me talk to Gus tomorrow and see what's happening in the investigation."

"She hasn't teamed up with you like she normally does?" That surprised me. Usually, my sister used Striker as a sounding board and an unofficial member of her detective squad.

"No, but then, she's had her hands full." Striker finished his slice and tilted the box in my direction.

"I'm all set."

"I better get going. Big day tomorrow."

I followed as he carried the remains of our pizza into the kitchen and shoved the box in my fridge before grabbing his jacket from the back of the chair where he'd tossed it when he came in. "We'll have to manage this business with Albert's ghost behind the scenes, of course."

"Of course. Gus would think we're crazy." I followed him to the door, leaning against the frame as he headed back out on the porch. Striker turned to face me, his gaze falling to my lips once more. He leaned in and brushed his lips against mine for a heart-stopping second before pulling away. He smelled of spicy cologne, and that scent became my new favorite. Heat prickled my cheeks as I did my best to focus on the case at hand and not the tingling awareness now zinging through my system. "Now that we know the real motive for the murder was that letter, hopefully, finding the killer will be easier. If you can just get Gus to follow the evidence Albert gave us, we should be all set."

"You make it sound so easy. It's never easy to get Gus to do anything."

"True, but I have faith. You can finagle things so she sees what she's supposed to. In the end, it's all about catching a killer."

"Yep." Striker paused, his eyes holding mine. "There's one thing even more important."

"What?"

"I always knew you were special, Chance, but now we both know that we're two of a kind."

13

The next morning, I sat with the regulars again, sipping my morning coffee and discussing the topic du jour: Albert's death. Pepper had stopped by to join us and pass out some kale-and-pistachio scones—a new recipe she was testing. They didn't go over too well, and we were all sitting around, politely trying to nibble at them without actually eating any.

I'd not slept well the night before, what with my mind racing with facts about that letter and also the fact that Striker could see the same ghosts I could. His parting words had warmed my heart but also made me nervous. Two of a kind... what exactly did that mean?

Truthfully, I'd felt so isolated since my accident and the appearance of my special "gift." To find out now that there was someone else who had the same ability, a man close to me whom I liked—okay, more than liked—was both encouraging and terrifying. Encouraging because I now had someone I could talk to about all these weird sightings, someone who would understand how creepy and compelling the spirits were, how I felt obligated to help them even when I didn't want to or when there might be personal danger involved. Someone who wouldn't think I was crazy or hysterical or making it all up just to get attention. Unfortunately, knowing Striker was more similar to me than I'd ever imagined was also terrifying because it meant that one of the huge barriers I'd set up between us to keep from allowing our relationship to develop further was now gone.

"I'm telling you, Ruthie said finding poor Albert dead on the steps and then finding out it wasn't an accident took ten years off her life," Josiah said, giving a shudder, his tone drawing me out of my thoughts and back into the conversation taking place around me. "The killer might have been right there, and Ruthie could have been in danger. As it was, she said she remembers hearing the squeal of tires as a car took off."

"You mean the killer was still there when she opened up?" I asked as I pictured the back steps of the post office. The back parking lot faced the front of the First Hope Church. Didn't Emma Potts or Pastor Foley get in early? If they did, then maybe they'd seen the car drive off.

Josiah nodded. "Yep. Least she thinks so. Heard a car drive off fast."

"I bet that was scary," Hattie Deering said, huddling farther down inside her cream-colored pantsuit. She and her sister, Cordelia, were wearing coordinating outfits of baby blue and cream. "It's a good thing the killer took off when they did, or Ruthie might've been next."

"True," Josiah agreed. He looked a tad better than he had the day before, some of his color returning to his wrinkled cheeks. His gray hair was combed over the top of his balding head, and he wore his normal brown tweed pants and sport coat. "Ruthie said she figured the murderer must've heard her unlocking the back door and that's what caused 'em to run off."

Pandora sat beside me on the purple sofa. I reached down to stroke her fur, and she peeked one eye open, her ears twitching as she listened to the conversation.

"Now that Gus has confirmed it was a deliberate act, I hope they start bringing in suspects," Cordelia said. "I'm betting that Barney Delaney will be at the top of their list, what with the tournament coming up and all."

"Oh, I don't know," I said, armed with the truth Albert had given me last night. Whoever had killed him had done so for the letter, not to win at checkers. "When Pepper and I went to the Schumers' house yesterday, that Desmond seemed like a shady character to me."

"Yes," Hattie agreed. "He's always been a no-good moocher. In fact, my niece told me that carpal tunnel injury claim of his is completely fake too. Got him out of work on paid disability."

"But he got a doctor to sign off on it, didn't he?" Pepper asked, frowning.

"Who knows how he accomplished that?" Hattie said, her tone dripping with distaste. "Much less perform the actual surgery on someone who doesn't even have carpal tunnel syndrome. Maybe he does have it a little, but I'm sure he's milking it."

"Sounds like a complicated mess to me," Bing said, standing and trying to discreetly wrap the remains of his scone in a napkin. "Too complicated for morning coffee. I'm off to run errands."

"Ah, Cordelia and I will go with you," Hattie said, pulling her sister to her feet beside her and eyeing their partially eaten scones. "We've got lots to get done today."

Cordelia looked at Pepper apologetically. "I think those scones need a bit more sugar."

"And less kale," Hattie added.

"And that's my cue to leave as well," Josiah said, tossing his empty cup and his scone in the trash before heading to the door with the others. "Have a good day, Willa. Pepper."

They all left in a flurry of bells and talking over each other, leaving my best friend and me to stare after them for a moment. Pandora stretched beside me on the sofa then promptly went back to sleep.

"So you didn't like your scone either?" Pepper looked at the scone in front of me. I'd taken one small bite and almost gagged. It had tasted like freshly mown grass.

"Let's say it needs a little work. Less kale was a good idea," I said. "Maybe kale isn't a great ingredient for scones?"

"Maybe." Pepper gathered up the scone remnants and threw them in the trash then changed the subject. "Did you see Albert's ghost again last night?"

"Yep. He said the killer was after the letter he had." I shifted my weight and stared down into my cup. "Striker was there too."

"Oh, did he bring dinner again?" Pepper watched me over the top of her tea, her eyes sparkling with mirth. "That makes what, twice this week already? Sounds like it's getting serious."

"You have no idea." I frowned. "He saw Albert too."

"Really?" She sipped her tea, not sounding a bit surprised. "Did you happen to share the dandelion tea with him that I gave you?"

"I did, actually. He tripped on his way into my house and hurt his knee. Why?"

"Well, in addition to its pain-relieving medicinal qualities, it also enhances second sight."

"Second sight?" I halted mid-sip.

"Yes." Pepper gave me a patient smile. "You know, seeing spirits. Of course, one has to have natural abilities to begin with..."

My suspicions rose higher by the second. I crossed my arms and stared across the table at my best friend, with a raised brow. Seemed last night's earth-shattering confessions hadn't been such a coincidence after all. "How convenient you gave me that tea yesterday, then, so I'd just happen to have it around the house when Striker came over and tripped. Did you set up Pandora running in front of him and getting tangled in his feet too?"

"Don't be ridiculous," Pepper said, sounding entirely too pleased with herself.

I gazed down at Pandora, who was now wide awake and looking up at me with a cat-who-ate-the canary expression. "And you," I said, scratching her belly. "I suppose you ran in front of him just to get him inside to drink my tea, eh?"

"Not to change the subject," Pepper said, though it was entirely clear that was exactly what she was doing, "but a local legend claims that Hester Warren sent a letter from her deathbed to one of her relatives, which contained information vital to preserving the peace and well-being of Mystic Notch. A letter that contains a list of ingredients she buried and hid from evildoers. If that legend turned out to be true and such a letter fell into the wrong hands, it could be very bad for everyone."

"Albert said the letter was from Helen Warren," I said.

"Her great-grandniece." Pepper sighed. "So the legend is true."

"It could have been just a regular letter," I said. "You know, the kind people write just to communicate and let someone know how they are doing."

But even as I said the words, I didn't think it had been. Somehow I knew it was the letter in the legend.

Normally, I would have thought that was stupid. What kind of letter could preserve the peace and well-being of a town? But a strange energy vibrated through me as I gazed into Pandora's eyes, a knowing, a certainty that what Pepper was telling me was true. When I was little, I'd believed in magic. My gram had instilled a sense of wonder in me. She'd told me tales of fairies and magical creatures. Kid stuff. After I'd left the Notch for college, all that wonder had gradually faded away. Then over my career as a journalist, I'd seen enough to dash any belief in fairies and magic I might have had.

Not to mention the bitter divorce and the accident that had nearly killed me. Both those things were enough to make it impossible to believe in the existence of magic. Yet those were the two things that had driven me back to Mystic Notch after Gram's death.

And now... Pandora climbed up onto my lap to put us face-to-face, and in my head, as crazy as it might sound, I heard her compelling me to believe. Believe in magic. Just like the message Adelaide's ghost had given me from Gram.

Considering the fact I talked to ghosts on a daily basis, I should've been more receptive, I suppose. And given that Striker, a law enforcement officer, sworn to protect and uphold the truth, had confessed to having the same ability, my doubts had taken a severe hit. Maybe magic wasn't such a far-fetched idea after all.

As if sensing the shift inside me, Pepper leaned forward and placed her hand over mine. "I can give you the ingredients for a charmed tea, one that makes people tell the truth. That way you can ask them point-blank about the letter."

Still a bit taken aback by it all, I shook my head. "But who would even know what was in that letter or that Albert had it?"

"Well, Desmond, for one." Pepper sat back and sighed. "Perhaps he'd even seen it when Albert dug it out of that old mailbag. And Desmond is usually in cahoots with Nathan Anderson. If it was the letter from Hester Warren and he told Nathan what he'd seen and they figured out its value, then maybe they decided to steal it and sell it off to the highest bidder."

"Barney did say that Desmond was in his shop, trying to sell him some of Albert's things right after the death." I scrunched my nose. "He said it was a stamp collection, though."

"Hmm." Pepper narrowed her eyes. "Or maybe Barney only thought it was a stamp collection. The letter would have had a stamp on it. Maybe Desmond only thought the stamp was valuable and not the letter inside. Then again, perhaps it was someone else.

Who knows how many people Albert might have mentioned the letter to?"

"Right." I set my cold coffee aside and pushed to my feet, wincing slightly at the ache in my leg. Pepper had been correct, though. The dandelion tea had helped. "I guess our next step is determining just who would know what was in the letter. Seems it'd be people who'd have ancestral lines dating back to old Hester's time. The only family I can think of like that in Mystic Notch is the Bateses."

Pepper scoffed. "Not just them. You'd be surprised how many townsfolk can trace their lineage back to one of Mystic Notch's original settlers—good or bad."

"So the town is full of suspects?"

"Not necessarily. The only person who would be interested enough to kill would be someone that wants harm to come to Mystic Notch."

"Oh well, that certainly narrows it down, then," I said. "We just have to find someone with malicious intent. I already have a few suspects in mind."

14

I was putting away books later that afternoon and feeling pretty good about myself and the store's future. I'd just sold a leather-bound edition of Robert Frost's poems worth a small fortune. It wasn't a huge amount, but it padded my coffers nicely. Things were looking up.

And speaking of looking up, I glanced at the clock on the wall behind the register for the umpteenth time. Once two o'clock rolled around, I planned to take a late lunch and head over to the church to talk with Emma Potts. She was the church secretary and had been working the day Albert Schumer was killed. Given that the church was right across the street from the back door of the post office, I'd hoped she might have seen something or someone suspicious on her way into work that day. Possibly even Felicity Bates, Desmond Lacroix, or Nathan Anderson. Those were my top suspects thus far.

Muffled conversation drew my attention to the far corner of the room, where my two resident spirits—Robert and Franklin—were deep in discussion. After making sure Hanna was busy helping customers and completely unaware of our ghostly visitors, I headed over to the poetry section, where the two undead men were conversing.

As I neared them, I couldn't help biting back a smile. Seemed I wasn't the only one as pleased as punch about my early sale.

"See?" Robert said, giving Franklin a superior look. "People still like to read my works."

Franklin snorted. "They still love to read my biographies too. But I don't think Willa promotes them enough." He waved a hand toward the section where his books were housed. "How can anyone be expected to find them when they're all pushed in like that so no one can see the titles?"

I cleared my throat and raised a brow as I tidied the aforementioned section. "A thank you for carrying both of your out-of-print books would be nice."

The two men exchanged a long-suffering look

before changing the subject, ignoring my suggestion entirely. Typical.

Robert sighed. "I heard you finally spoke with Albert. The disturbances on the other side have lessened."

"Yes." Franklin leaned a ghostly shoulder against the bookshelf beside him. It sank right through, causing him to stumble slightly and right himself. Expression perturbed, he narrowed his gaze on me. "I also heard that your young man talked to Albert as well. About time you two connected."

At first, I thought they were talking about me connecting with Albert, but then Franklin's words finally registered. I halted with a book halfway into its slot. "Wait a minute. You knew about Striker's gift? That means each time he came in here, he could see you too, then."

"No." Robert held up his hands against my accusing tone. "It doesn't work like that. Yes, we knew about your Striker's abilities, but the only person who can see the two of us in here is you, Willa."

"Hmm." I continued shoving books onto the shelf, feeling slightly off-kilter now. Who else knew Striker and I could see ghosts?

Robert and Franklin stood watching me as I worked, both looking contrite. Finally, I took pity on them and ended the awkward silence stretching between us. "Albert was quite forthcoming with information. And I'm glad for you both that the disturbances are growing less annoying now that we're investigating what happened. But I do wish Albert remembered the identity of his killer. It would make things so much easier."

"Unfortunately, they never do." Robert shook his head. "It's called death amnesia. The memories are too painful to remember at that exact moment, so most ghosts block them out."

"Huh." I finished putting the stack of books in my arms away then peered around the corner of the bookcase to make sure Hanna was still occupied before saying, "Josiah said this morning that Ruthie scared off Albert's killer, but she swears she didn't see who it was. That's why I'm going over to First Hope Church now. I want to talk to Emma Potts and Pastor Foley too, if he's there. It's possible they might have seen something on their way in that morning."

"An excellent idea," Franklin said. "Perhaps you could—"

Whatever he'd been about to suggest was cut off by my sister storming into the store. I battled the urge to hide in the corner and instead squared my shoulders. Putting off the inevitable wouldn't make it go away.

After a quick glance at my two ghost friends, I stepped out from between the bookshelves to face Gus head on. "Good afternoon, sis. What can I do for you?"

"You can start off by telling me what in the world you said to Striker."

I did my best to keep the guilt from my face and failed miserably, if my sister's narrowed gaze was any indication. Aware that there were customers in the store and that we were drawing their attention, I guided Gus over to a secluded corner before continuing. "Why? What's wrong with him?"

"Nothing, except he used to be normal. Now he can't stop talking about strange suspects that never crossed our rosters before and weird alibis." Gus huffed. "Not to mention some old letter. And stop bothering Barney Delaney. He was in my office this morning, reading me the riot act and threatening to file charges against you for harassment. He had nothing to do with this, Willa, okay? I already talked to him, and he was at the diner, having breakfast during the time Albert was killed. Just like he is every morning. There are witnesses, and Myrna showed me his time-stamped receipt for 5:57 a.m. and everything. Got it?"

Whenever my sister got into a tizzy like this, it was best to just go along with it until she calmed down. So

I nodded and gave her my best placating smile. "Fine. No more Barney Delaney. I promise. Though you might want to check into Desmond Lacroix and Nathan Anderson. Were you aware they both tried to sell Albert's stamp collection to Barney on the day Albert died?"

Gus's expression turned mulish, and my hopes sank. Stubbornness was a family trait with us Chances, but my sister took it to a whole new level. She didn't like me butting in to her investigations. I got that. But that didn't make my information any less valid.

"Listen, Willa. I don't like this. I've made it abundantly clear you can't go poking around my cases. I know how to do my job, and I don't need you or anyone else telling me what's what."

Before I could say anything else, Gus blustered out of the shop, leaving me and my customers to stare after her. Luckily, my phone buzzed, giving me an excuse to escape behind the counter and avoid any more mortifying situations. Nothing like fighting with your sibling in front of the world. I pulled out my cell, relieved to see Striker's name on my caller ID. I answered, leaning against the wall, my cheeks hot and my breath rapid. "Hello?"

"Hey," he said, his deep voice like a balm to my unease. "You okay, Chance?"

"Yeah, I'm fine," I lied. "What's up?"

"Well, since it's such a nice day outside, I was wondering if you might like to have an early dinner with me this afternoon. I thought maybe we could pick up some takeout at the diner and have an impromptu picnic in the park in town. Gus needs me to work a shift for her tonight, so I won't be around then."

"Oh, um. Okay." My shoulders slumped, some of my tension leaving. "That sounds good. I haven't had lunch, so I'll just wait and eat with you later. What time?"

"Four thirty too late?"

"Nope. Sounds good." I checked the clock on my desk. "Perfect, actually. I've got an errand to run before then, so we can discuss Albert's case over our meal."

"Great." I could hear the smile in his voice, and my toes curled in my shoes despite my wishes to the contrary. He was just so darned charming and kind and wonderful. "I'll see you then. You want me to pick up some sandwiches?"

"Yep."

"Awesome. See you at four thirty."

"See you." Warm fuzzies filled me as I ended the call then grinned like an idiot.

I gathered my purse and tiptoed past Pandora, who was laying on her cat bed in the window, on my way to the front door. I'd wanted to head over to the church without her, but that never worked out well. Somehow my cat seemed to have a sixth sense about my leaving and always followed. I didn't want to take the chance of her navigating the streets of Mystic Notch by herself, so I figured I'd take her along with me.

But when I checked, Pandora was sound asleep.

Maybe, for once, I could go somewhere on my own. I headed down the cookbook aisle to tell Hanna where I was going. Then I slipped out the back door of the shop and headed for First Hope.

15

Pandora opened her eyes as soon as she heard the door shut behind Willa. A quick glance around showed Hanna busy with a customer, making it the perfect time to escape. She climbed out of her warm sherpa-lined bed and had a good stretch before taking off for the storage closet in the back of the store and the secret opening inside of it that led outside. After a few strategically placed bats of her paw on the door, the storage closet creaked open, and Pandora disappeared inside.

She zipped around various mops, buckets, and brooms to the far corner then slipped behind a box of cleaning supplies and into the tight tunnel through the wall. With a bit of squeezing, she soon emerged out into the alley beside the shop, where the warm sunshine directly opposed the chilly breeze ruffling her fur.

From there, she sped toward the woods at the edge of Mystic Notch, where her seventh sense had told her the other cats would be meeting. She was excited to share her updates on her plans to get Willa focused on finding the killer and how she brought her human and Striker's talents together. She hoped the others had been as lucky as well and they could get this murder mess wrapped up sooner than expected.

Near the edge of Elspeth's property, just outside the barn, she found the other felines waiting. Otis was there, along with Inkspot and Tigger. Beside Tigger sat Truffles—a small tortoiseshell cat with black-and-orange mottled fur and eerie greenish-yellow eyes.

Pandora made her way around the circle, sniffing and greeting each cat in turn, before settling into a spot beside Sasha to listen. Conversations were already underway.

"Well, I've been following people all day," Truffles said, "trying to figure out who's the killer."

"Same here," Sasha said. "No luck so far."

"You cats are going about this all wrong," Otis said, shifting his sizable bulk. "If Albert was killed trying to deliver that note, then whoever did it will surely have started recovering ingredients in order to reverse the pleasantry charm by now. You look for evidence of that, and you'll find your human."

"What evidence?" Hope, a young chimera cat whose

half-orange, half-black face was divided exactly down the middle of her nose, asked. Her eyes, one blue and one green, looked curiously at Otis.

"Well, digging, I suppose. If Hester buried the ingredients, then the human would be digging. We should be able to raise our senses and smell the freshly turned earth mixed with the scent of a cover-up."

"Speaking of humans," Inkspot said in his deep, rumbling voice. "How are things going with your human, Pandora?"

"Better than expected." She licked her paw to avoid looking too proud of herself. "She's coming along nicely. I was able to get her to imbibe the dandelion tea and speak with Albert's ghost directly. I also got her and the other human, Striker, to join together with their powers. They should be able to find the murderer any day now, as they will be more powerful with their forces combined."

Otis scoffed. "Sounds doubtful to me."

Gaze narrowed, Pandora gave her nemesis a measured stare. Despite their differences, having that pleasantry charm lifted would make life harder for all of them. Given Otis's penchant for lying around and being lazy, she couldn't imagine he'd like his days inconvenienced in any way. Especially not by having to run around the Notch and babysit humans who were bickering and turning to evil deeds. Therefore, he must be rooting for her to succeed deep down inside. She took comfort in that idea and decided not to whap him hard with her paw for being nasty.

"I didn't know Striker could see ghosts too," Truffles said. "Then again, you're the only feline amongst us who can also talk to the spirits, so if anyone would know, it would be you, Pandora."

"True." Pandora gave a slight shake of her head. "I think I'm making good headway with Striker too. He seems a bit more receptive to my suggestions than Willa."

"While some *of us spend their time manipulating weak-minded humans," Otis said, his tone as grating as always, "others of us are trying to solve this case. We need results and fast."*

"Me-yow!" Kelley yelped from the shadows, and all eyes turned to her as she trotted into the group. She sat down, curling her tail around her haunches, and Pandora noticed the poor thing's tail was covered in brambles and burrs. That looked as painful as heck.

"What happened?" Inkspot asked.

"I have news. I ran all the way from the river, through Farmer Duffy's field."

"The field?" Sasha's blue eyes were wide. "But you know that place is full of burrs and brambles."

"I know." Kelley looked at her tail. "But I did not want to waste time. The news is of the utmost importance. The killer has already started digging up the first ingredient."

"The first ingredient?" Truffles said. "What is it?"

"Eye of newt?" Otis asked.

"Raindrops from the petals of the foxglove plant?" Sasha suggested.

"Salamander legs?" Tigger said.

"I have no idea what it is." Kelley gingerly tried to comb out her mangled tail, wincing. "All I saw when I was in the woods was the hole the killer left behind. I smelled their desperation and victory, and there was a subtle scent of ancient times."

"Ancient times?" Inkspot's voice was a low growl. "Then it must have been one of the ingredients."

"Whatever they took had been kept in a jar too. The glass had been smashed everywhere. It's a wonder I didn't cut my paw trying to get out of there. Whoever killed Albert wasn't so lucky. I smelled their blood—O positive."

"That doesn't help at all." Otis scowled. "That's the most common type in humans."

"Maybe it will be of assistance," Inkspot said, wandering over to help Kelley with her matted fur. "At least we now have one clue. We can be on the lookout for a human with a cut or scratch from the glass."

"Does anyone know how many ingredients are in the charm?" Pandora asked.

The others shook their heads.

"I'd say anywhere from five to ten. That seems pretty typical for a charm," Tigger said.

"And the killer only has one?" Sasha straightened. "That should give us a little time."

"We don't know for sure how many the killer has," Otis said. "No telling where the rest might be hidden either. I doubt that the human, Hester Warren, was dumb enough to bury them all in the same place. She'd scatter them around, hide them in different places. For all we know, the rest could just be sitting somewhere on a shelf in an old building." He gave Pandora an assessing look. "Maybe even stowed away in a church or with those musty old books your human loves so much."

"I think our best bet at this point is to break up into groups," Inkspot said, his tone commanding. "Each pair will follow a suspect. There is Nathan Anderson, Felicity Bates, Desmond Lacroix. Time is of the essence. We need to discover the identity of the killer before they find all the ingredients, or there's no telling what will happen."

16

I walked down the street to First Hope Church. From the exterior, it didn't look like much—boxy and white. Once I was inside, it took my eyes a few minutes to adjust to the dimmer light, and I blinked hard to clear my vision. Eventually, I could make out rows of dark oak pews lining the sides of the space. Light spilled in from the large, round stained-glass window set high in the gable at the far end of the church, casting a rainbow of colors across the modest altar.

Frosted rectangular windows with rounded tops were spaced along the walls, but they didn't let in a lot of light. The air was as quiet as a library and smelled of candle wax and sweet incense. To the left of the altar, three rows of small confessional candles flickered. The candles were a new addition to the church and added to the soothing ambiance.

My footsteps echoed across the empty church as I walked down the marble center aisle on the way to the back, where the office was. That was where I figured I'd find Emma or Pastor Foley.

I'd figured right. Emma was in the office, sorting through a box of candles. She glanced up as I appeared in the doorway.

"Willa! What a nice surprise. What can I help you with today?"

"Hi," I said, smoothing a hand down my jeans. "I wondered if I could talk to you a few minutes."

"Oh, well, I suppose so," Emma said, waving me into her office. "I could stand a little break."

"Great, thanks." I stepped inside the tiny room and took a seat in the chair in front of her desk. She was a petite, older lady with gray hair and horn-rimmed glasses. I refused the tea she offered and waited until she settled into her seat once more before asking, "I wondered if you remembered seeing anyone lurking around these parts the morning Albert Schumer was killed."

"Hmm." Emma gave me a thoughtful look. "Funny you should ask. Your sister was in here earlier, wanting to know the same thing. I'll tell you what I told her.

The only person I saw in the vicinity that day was Nathan Anderson. He drove away from the post office about six in the morning. I know the time exactly because our bells chime exactly on the hour. I come in before six just to hear them. Plus, I can walk into the narthex and see the sun rising through the stained glass. It's really beautiful. I saw his car through the glass in the front doors."

"Sounds like it," I said, smiling. "Are you sure it was Nathan Anderson?"

"Absolutely. He drives a silver Prius with a little ding on the passenger-side door. No mistaking it." Emma leaned closer and whispered, "Plus, I know I'm not supposed to say this, but Nathan is a friend of the feral cats, like you. So, I feel like I can talk about it since we're alone."

"Huh." After seeing Nathan arguing with Felicity Bates, I'd had him pegged as a villain. But hearing that the guy helped take care of the feral cat population of Mystic Notch made me reconsider.

Mystic Notch had a large population of wild cats. We'd tried to rehome them, but some of them just could not be caught. We did our best to keep them fed and cared for. We sort of acted like a secret society, anonymous and all, bringing food and other supplies to secret shelter locations all around town.

There were a lot of vocal people in the area who'd love nothing more than to do away with all the lost and abandoned cats, so we moved locations frequently to avoid discovery. I hoped that Emma was right and that Nathan was a true and kind friend to the local feral population and hadn't infiltrated our group to do harm. But if he was a kind friend, then why was he running from Albert Schumer's dead body?

"And you didn't see anyone else that morning?"

"No, dear." Emma sat back and straightened her already-pristine desktop. "Only a few of us early risers are up and about that time of the morning. Usually just me, Pastor Foley, the postmaster, and the good Lord above."

"Okay, then." I pushed to my feet and headed for the door. "Well, thank you for talking to me, Emma. Have a nice afternoon."

"Thank you, Willa. You do the same." Emma slid her glasses up her nose and picked up a stack of papers, her attention firmly focused on her work once more. There was no sign of Pastor Foley around the church, so I decided to leave for my late lunch with Striker a bit sooner than expected. I could take a leisurely walk through town beforehand and stew over the new information I'd just learned.

I stepped back out into the bright sunshine and

stood for a minute, enjoying the late-autumn day and the sounds of leaves rustling around my feet. I should be happy Emma had seen the person that Ruthie had heard fleeing that morning. According to what I'd heard, Nathan was into something with Desmond. It was possible he'd learned about the letter from Desmond when Desmond wanted to sell it for the stamp. The letter was old, so the stamp must have had some value, and if Albert didn't think so and if the letter was never mailed, it wouldn't have been postmarked either, thus making it worth more.

But now that I knew Nathan helped take care of the cats, I wasn't so sure he was the killer. Then again, Nathan was friendly with Felicity. Or was he? I'd seen them arguing in front of my shop, and that would seem to indicate they were not on friendly terms.

Emma's sighting didn't conclusively prove that Nathan Anderson had killed Albert Schumer. But despite his supposed charity toward stray cats, why else would the man be driving away from the back of the post office where a dead body was sprawled on the steps if it wasn't because he was fleeing with the letter Albert had been carrying?

17

Staring around the church parking lot, I moved to where Emma had said she was standing at the time she spotted Nathan's car, and tried to figure out where the vehicle might have come from if not the post office. My conscience still required me to give him the benefit of the doubt until proven guilty. However, it was clear the post office was the only reasonable conclusion since the only other business on the street was the diner, but it wasn't nearby, and for Nathan, driving past the church lot would've been well out of his way.

I walked back to the bookstore and entered to find Pandora sleeping in the same spot in her cat bed as when I'd left earlier. My suspicions rose. Usually, the cat got angry when I went somewhere without her.

And when Pandora was angry, she liked to express it by messing with things.

I made a quick inspection of the shop, searching for hairballs or shredded toilet paper strewn about like streamers. Nothing. Frowning, I made my way back to the front of the store and chatted with Hanna while I stowed my purse under the counter. She hadn't noticed Pandora doing anything nasty, and as far as she knew, the cat had snoozed in her fluffy bed the whole time I'd been gone other than one trip to the litter box in the storage closet.

Maybe Pandora was tired. After all, she'd been up to a lot the night before, getting Striker and me to drink that dandelion tea then confess our secret abilities to one another. And I still couldn't shake the fact I'd *heard* her thoughts inside my head. Not like the usual, "Oh, I bet this is what my cat's thinking" sort of thing either. No. The more I'd thought about it, the more I was convinced that Pandora was trying to communicate with me, telepathically.

A glance at the clock showed it was a quarter after three. My picnic date with Striker in the park was at four thirty, so I had a little bit of time to get some paperwork sorted here at the shop and help out with reshelving and other things. Hanna had already left for the day, but since there were no customers in sight, I didn't mind closing a little early.

I'd just gathered a stack of returned books in my arms to carry them across the room when the bells jangled above the door. I peered around the end of the aisle to see Barney Delaney standing at the counter.

Setting the books aside, I forced a polite smile. "Hello, Barney. What can I help you with today?"

"I'm looking for a reference book on Canadian coins," he said, his voice as gruff as his expression. "Figured you might have it. I had a customer bring a collection in, and I need to look up some things."

"Ah." I led him over to the section he needed, noticing a silver Prius driving slowly past on the street outside the shop. From where I was standing, it appeared the shadowy driver was trying to peer inside the bookstore. I squinted and saw a ding on the passenger-side door, and my feet fumbled.

Was that Nathan Anderson? Worse, was he here *with* Barney? I braced a hand against a nearby bookshelf for balance and tried to calm my racing heart as I pointed to the reference books I currently had in stock. "This is all I've got right now, I'm afraid. Usually when you need something, you call me first so I can see if I've got what you need or can order it, Barney."

"There wasn't time. Client just dropped them off,

and I need to evaluate them in a hurry. My books don't have these Canadian coins listed. Let's see. I brought one over..." He pulled out a large tome and scowled as he flipped through it then took a small packet, which I assumed contained the coin, out of his pocket. He was already wearing the white cotton gloves one used to avoid getting oils on valuable coins, and he took it out of the pouch to compare. "You heard anything new about the murder?"

There were any number of reasons why he might be asking. He and Albert had been friends, after all. The fact that a silver Prius just like Nathan Anderson's had driven by moments earlier could be pure coincidence.

"Uh, nope. Just what everyone else around here has heard. Why?"

"I want this thing resolved." Barney scanned the pages of the book, searching intently for something. "My gut tells me that Desmond Lacroix was taking advantage of Albert and that Nathan Anderson was involved somehow. That Anderson might've come from an old family with old money, but most of it's gone now. I'd wager that's why he's been sniffing around the Bates family these days, trying to get them to invest in stamps and commodities."

His unexpected answer got my attention. I crossed

my arms and stood a bit firmer. "Stamps and commodities? Can you be a bit more specific?"

Barney looked up then, as if just realizing what he'd let slip. His gaze darted away then, and he reached into his back pocket for his wallet. "Sorry. No, I can't. Really don't want to cast aspersions on anyone." He switched the book to his other hand and tried his other back pocket. Then he cursed softly under his breath. "Seems I forgot my wallet."

"Oh. Just take it." I stepped back slowly from him, glancing over at Pandora, who still appeared to be sleeping soundly in her bed. Normally inquisitive, she was usually the first one to greet customers when they came in, but not this afternoon. Was she ill? I looked back at Barney, who was watching me with an unreadable expression. "Seriously. You can pay me for it later. It's not like I don't know where to find you."

My joke fell flat.

Barney shuffled toward the exit, mumbling his thanks as he passed.

Barney sure was an odd duck. And Nathan driving by made me nervous. Things were getting weird, but I didn't have time to mull that over. It was time to meet Striker, and I was starving.

18

The small park near the center of town was usually very private. Mystic Notch wasn't exactly a hotbed of activity. Sure, we got a good amount of tourist traffic in the summer, but now that it was past peak foliage season, things were slow. Fine by me. It meant a more private late lunch with Striker. We'd be able to talk about Albert without anyone overhearing.

Today had been strange all around. Poor Pandora still wasn't acting right either. She hadn't even meowed when I'd left to meet Striker. She'd barely lifter her head at all. Usually, she'd be trying to sneak out the door behind me. If things didn't improve by tonight, I'd call the vet and make an appointment for her. I glanced back at the front of the bookstore and was relieved to see her open at least one greenish-gold orb to watch me from her spot in the window. Maybe once she saw me walk away, she'd start clawing at the door in her usual fashion.

I crossed the street and walked down a block to the park. The trees were almost bare now, and it was easy to spot Striker at a picnic table near a small copse of pines at the far corner of the space. As I got closer, I saw that he'd laid out a whole spread of food. Forget the sandwiches he'd mentioned earlier. There was fried chicken and coleslaw, rolls and butter, mashed potatoes, and even corn.

"Hey," he said, his gray eyes warm as I approached. "I wasn't sure what you wanted from the diner, so I got a bit of everything on special." The corners of his eyes crinkled when he smiled, and tiny flutters of attraction took flight inside me. I slid onto the bench across from him and set my purse beside me before filling my plate with goodies.

"How's your day going?" Striker asked, tearing into a chicken leg.

"Weird," I answered truthfully. I filled him in on Barney Delaney's recent visit to my shop as I buttered a roll. "He thinks Desmond's got something to do with Albert's death."

"Can't." Striker polished off his chicken leg then

grabbed another from the box. "Guy's got an airtight alibi. He was at the emergency clinic the morning Albert Schumer died. Doctor and nurse both verify that he was there, having his stitches looked at. Seems they were getting infected."

"Could he have faked it?" I nibbled on a chunk of chicken breast. The deep-fried breading was salty and spicy and melted in my mouth, while the chicken was tender and succulent. Score another winner for the local diner. "Or maybe he rushed over there after killing Albert."

"Nah." Striker wiped his hands then pulled out his trusty notebook from his pocket and flipped through it. "No way. The clinic told me they log everything into their computer, and the medical records show Lacroix was with Dr. Green at five forty-five, the time of Albert's death."

"Hmm." I took a bite of creamy mashed potatoes, frowning. "You think his injury is real?"

"Would have to be, unless Dr. Green is lying too." Striker shrugged and took a sip from his water bottle. "Since you and I have a special 'in' with Albert, perhaps we can ask him if Desmond really had carpal tunnel the next time we see him." He winked at me. "My knee's still aching from that fall the other night, so more of Pepper's tea would be in order."

I smiled, genuinely this time, enjoying the warm tingles of companionship I felt around him now. We'd gotten off to a rocky start, what with Striker thinking I was a criminal and all the first time we'd met, but the truth was I'd always been attracted to him. And I think the feeling was mutual. We'd been dating ever since. And now, apparently, we were trying to solve murders together. I made a mental note to try to conjure up Albert's ghost so I could ask him about Desmond. While I was at it, I'd ask about the argument with Barney too. What if this whole thing had nothing to do with Hester Warren's letter and he'd argued with Barney that morning again and it had turned deadly?

But no matter what his answer, my money was on Nathan and Felicity. After all, Emma had seen Nathan's car leaving the scene of the crime.

Now—with our shared "talents"—I felt closer to Striker than ever. "Yeah, maybe." I took a bite of corn, savoring its sweet, buttery flavor. "I walked over and talked to Emma Potts this morning too. She said she saw Nathan Anderson driving away from the post office around the time Albert was murdered. Since Ruthie scared whoever did the deed away, maybe Nathan is guilty."

"Nathan Anderson, huh?" Striker narrowed his

gaze. "That's odd. He called in right before I left to come here. Reported a break-in at his shed."

"Oh really? He drove by my shop really slowly when Barney was in there. I recognized the car from Emma's description."

Striker made a face. "There could be more than one person with the same car."

"Don't think so. His had a dent on the passenger-side door."

"Hmm... well, I'll see if I can sway Gus into digging deeper into him. I did tell her you heard him arguing with Felicity about a letter. Killing someone to steal something of value out of their hand is motive."

"And I wouldn't put it past Felicity to get Nathan to do her dirty work then screw him over when it came time for the payoff. That's probably what the argument was about." I finished my roll, contemplating whether I should mention the pleasantry charm or not, then decided why not? After all, Striker could see ghosts just like me. Odds were good he wouldn't find the possibility of magic being real that weird, right? I finished the last of my food then pushed my plate away to rest my clasped hands on the tabletop. "Pepper mentioned that the letter Albert had could've been a list of ingredients."

"Ingredients for what?" Striker asked as he packed up our trash and tossed it in a nearby bin.

I took a deep breath before answering. "A spell."

"A spell, huh?" Striker took his seat again, toying with his water bottle and not meeting my gaze. If he thought there was anything strange about what I'd said, he didn't show it. "What kind of spell?"

"A pleasantry charm, from what I've been told. Meant to keep the peace around town. Pepper said that if someone was able to assemble all of the ingredients on the list, they could break the charm and cause havoc in Mystic Notch." I squeezed my hands tighter together. "What if Nathan's been digging for the ingredients and called in a break-in to cover up ahead of time?"

"Cover up?"

"Yeah, you know, if his shovel is found at the scene of the digging or something."

"Hmm... that doesn't make much sense. We wouldn't be investigating digging during the course of investigating Albert's death. The police wouldn't know about this charm or the ingredients, and his digging wouldn't be linked to the murder."

Dang, he was right. "I guess. Does he have an alibi for the time of Albert's murder?"

"Not according to Gus." Striker sighed, his frown deepening.

"Gus checked his alibi?" I was surprised. If that was true, my sister had taken the information I'd passed along through Striker about Nathan Anderson seriously and had looked into him. Maybe she did value my opinions more than she let on.

"So how does Felicity fit in if Nathan is doing the digging?"

"He could be her minion. We know she thinks she's a witch and would be after the ingredients." I shrugged. "Maybe she put a spell on him or is paying him. I really don't know much about witches and magic, to tell you the truth."

"If this spell thing Pepper told you about is real, then we need to find not only the killer, but also this letter and make sure whoever would want to dig up the ingredients is not able to do that. That's gonna make it harder, especially if Felicity is getting Nathan to do her dirty work. We might not find physical evidence to tie her to the crime."

I checked my watch then stood. "I need to get back to the bookstore. But I will say that the best way to get my sister to go along with your ideas is to make her think it was her idea to begin with." Striker laughed, and I smiled then added, "Believe me. I've had tons of experience."

"I believe you, Chance." His use of my nickname sent a fresh wave of happiness tingling through me. We walked slowly back across the park. "Since I'm working a shift with her tonight at the police station, I'll try to figure out a way to do that."

"And I'll try to get Albert to tell me more about Desmond and the argument with Barney. Maybe it will at least let us rule them out. Then we can work on getting actual evidence against Felicity and Nathan."

"Just promise you'll be careful, Chance," Striker said, facing me as we waited at the corner. "We need to be able to prove our suspect had means, motive, and opportunity beyond a whisper of a doubt before we present it to Gus. Otherwise, she won't believe it, and we need to catch the person responsible soon, before things get uglier than they already are."

19

Pandora wished Willa were on board with the magical goings-on in Mystic Notch and the important roles the cats played. Pretending to be fast asleep in her cat bed so Willa wouldn't take her somewhere when she needed to sneak out was getting tedious.

Pandora opened one eye and watched Willa walk down the street from the comfort of her cat bed. Her seventh sense had told her to meet the cats outside the Bates mansion. They were tailing Felicity Bates this afternoon to see if she was the one digging up ingredients, and Pandora didn't want to miss out. She waited until Willa was out of sight then ran for her escape route in the closet.

Pandora raced across town, slowing to a trot only once she'd scurried under the imposing black wrought-iron fence on the edge of the Bates property. Up ahead, Otis, Sasha,

Tigger, and Hope were crouched down in the field, watching the house.

She weaved her way through the tall grasses, keeping one eye on the foreboding mansion that loomed in the distance as she made her way toward the cats. The Bates mansion was like something out of a gothic movie—all turrets and widows' walks and eyebrow windows that gave you the impression the house was watching you. Pandora suppressed a shiver and let the late-afternoon sunshine warm her fur as she breathed deep the earthy scent of freshly fallen leaves. The breeze tickled her whiskers as she came up to the group.

Otis turned around. "It's about time you got here. What's wrong? Did your human keep you cooped up?"

Pandora bristled. Did he always have to make a snide comment? She couldn't help but retaliate. "At least I have a human all to myself."

"Stop with the arguing. We're on a mission," Hope said. She was the youngest of the group but already very wise. Pandora knew she was destined for greatness and had already shown an aptitude for leadership. Perhaps one day, if Inkspot decided to step down, Hope would take his place.

"Where are the others?" Pandora asked.

"They're looking for signs of digging around town. We've only discovered one of the relics. We don't know how

many have been dug up. They're raising their seventh senses together to sniff it out."

The cats' extraordinary senses were made more powerful when they focused in a group, especially their seventh sense, which allowed them to hone in on something specific.

Pandora settled down on her haunches. "So what's happened with Felicity?"

"Nothing," Tigger said. "We followed her for hours, and all she has done is get her nails done and go clothes shopping."

"All this running around town is exhausting," Otis said.

"Maybe if you lost some weight, you could keep up." The words were out of Pandora's mouth before she could stop them, and she regretted them immediately when Hope speared her with an angry look. She really shouldn't lower herself to Otis's level, but she just couldn't help herself.

"Anyway, we raised our seventh senses while we were here, and there's no sign of the letter in the house. Or the ingredients," Sasha said.

"But it has to be Felicity," Pandora said. "I heard her arguing with Nathan Anderson outside the bookstore."

"Arguing?" Otis frowned.

"Yes, about the letter."

"If they were arguing, that means they might not *be in*

on this together," Hope said. "What exactly were they saying?"

Pandora thought about it. She'd only heard mention of the letter, then Fluff had jumped in the window and distracted her. "I'm not sure, but they were definitely at odds."

The cats exchanged an uneasy glance.

"Perhaps one of them has it, and the other is trying to take it," Sasha said.

"Yeah, but which one?" Otis asked.

Hope held up a paw. "Shh. I think I hear something."

Hiss!

Pandora leapt at the sound behind her, her heart slamming against her rib cage when she saw a giant, white, fluffy ball. Fluff.

The cats all jumped back, and Pandora instinctively put her body between Fluff and Hope. Pandora and Hope had done battle with Fluff before, and Fluff's powers were strong. Fluff had tried once to force Hope over to the side of evil, and Pandora could tell by the predatory gleam in Fluff's orange eyes as his gaze fell upon Hope that he wasn't done trying. He had almost succeeded before, and Pandora shuddered to think of what might happen if he had.

Hope stood tall and stepped out from behind Pandora. She had grown a lot since the battle. Maybe now Fluff *would be no match for her. Fluff might have been thinking the same. He shrank back just the tiniest bit.*

"What are you malcontents doing out here? This is private property," Fluff hissed.

"What are you going to do? Call the cops?" Tigger asked.

Fluff glared at him, and Tigger inched back half a paw.

"You people shouldn't be spying. Soon all your goody-two-shoes ways will be for nothing. And you'll be sorry that you crossed me." Fluff's gaze fell on Hope again. "Though there is still time for some of you to come over to my side."

"Not on your life," Hope said.

"Have it your way, then. You'll soon see what happens when things are not so pleasant in Mystic Notch."

Pandora's blood chilled, and she glanced uneasily at the others. Their ears were angled forward, their whiskers twitching.

"What do you mean?" Otis asked.

"You know what I mean." Fluff sat back on his haunches. "The reversal of the pleasantry charm."

"Before it can be reversed, all the ingredients need to be recovered," Hope said.

"Of course." Fluff licked his paw and ran it behind his pink-and-white ear.

"And your human does not seem to be the type to dig," Otis added, eliciting a scorching look from Fluff.

"Neither does yours. In fact, she's an old lady. Very old. I highly doubt she's up for digging."

Otis drew himself up taller. "My human has more magic in her little finger than yours does in her whole body!"

"Yeah, we'll see what good that does her once my human finds all the ingredients. Then she will be able to reverse the pleasantry charm, and Mystic Notch will be ours. In fact, I hear your human is quite ancient. Perhaps only the good and pleasant magic is keeping her alive. What do you think will happen to her once the charm is reversed? As soon as my human finds the let—" Fluff snapped his mouth shut and looked around nervously.

Otis pounced on his words "Aha! So your human does not have the letter!"

Fluff frowned. "What? No. I didn't say that she didn't have it."

"You didn't have to, because if she did, she'd surely be digging up the ingredients right now," Hope said, glancing at the house. "And from what we can tell, she hasn't done any digging, unless you consider rummaging in the sale rack at Ducharme's department store digging."

Fluff's whiskers twitched, and he glared at the cats.

"Fine then. But yours must not have it either if you are here looking for it."

"Well, fine then!" Otis arched his back and stepped closer to Fluff. Pandora had only seen him exhibit bravery once before, but she knew he had it in him. Otis was more complicated than he let on. She had a sneaking suspicion his ornery and uncaring demeanor was just for show, and she vowed to be less antagonistic toward him. That might not last long, but at least she'd try.

The cats all glared at each other, the only sound a few guttural growls and an odd hiss here and there.

After a few seconds, Fluff stood. "Okay. I'll give it to you that neither one of us has the letter. But that's okay, my friends, because now it's game on. Whoever finds the letter first will be the winner, and unlike your band of strays, I am no loser." And with that, he presented his backside and stalked off toward the house, his fluffy tail high in the air.

"Well, I guess that answers the question. Felicity does not have the letter," Otis said.

"Then that means she's not the killer," Sasha said.

"Then who is?" Pandora wondered.

"Is it Nathan? Desmond?"

"What about the wife?" Tigger asked, and everyone turned to him in surprise.

"The wife?" Otis asked.

Tigger grimaced. "Well, sometimes when I watch television with Elspeth in the house, she likes to watch detective shows, and it's usually the spouse that did it."

"I do not think that is the case here," Hope said gently.

Tigger looked down at the ground. "Probably not. There is much more at stake here than spousal jealousy or anger."

Hope turned to Pandora. "You heard Nathan and Felicity arguing about the letter. Perhaps Nathan is the one we should look into next. Felicity was likely trying to get him to hand it over."

"I heard that Desmond was working with Nathan," Sasha said.

"Desmond would have known about the letter because he was related to Albert," Tigger added.

"Maybe they are all in it together?" Sasha suggested.

"There is another one who might have known about the letter," Otis said. "The antique dealer, Barney Delaney. One of the feral cats said they heard him arguing with Albert, and Albert's son-in-law, Desmond, was seen in Barney's shop. Perhaps they are working together."

Pandora remembered the bookstore regulars talking about Barney Delaney and how he would likely win the checkers contest now. "Perhaps Albert's death had nothing to do with the letter and more to do with anger. Barney may have killed him over an argument or their rivalry at checkers."

Tigger's whiskers twitched. "But you said yourself that Felicity knows about the letter. Seems more likely that is the reason for Albert's death. And we know it was taken from his body."

"Good point, Pandora, but my vote is on Nathan," Otis said. "His family goes way back to Hester's time, and he clearly knows about the letter if he was arguing with Felicity."

Pandora's heart warmed at Otis's words. Apparently, he did trust her judgment.

Hope stood and started toward the edge of the field, the others following. "We have many suspects to follow. Let us go back to the barn and see if the others have found more evidence of digging."

"And take a catnap," Otis added. "We need to be fresh to follow these suspects, as things could get dangerous."

"Good point," Sasha said. "I vote we stick together from here on in. We are more powerful in numbers."

"We'll confer with the others as to which suspect to start with." Otis glanced at Pandora. "But from what we've heard, maybe Pandora is right, and it should be Nathan Anderson."

20

I returned from my late lunch with Striker to find Pandora still asleep in her bed. Apparently, she'd slept the whole time, as I didn't find signs of any mischief in the shop. She looked completely exhausted and was barely able to trot out to the car for the ride home. I worried once again if something was wrong with her. Should I make a vet appointment?

"What's with you, Pandora? Are you coming down with something?" Did cats come down with colds like people? I'd had Pandora for several years and hadn't known her to get sick once. "You're acting like you've been out running around all afternoon instead of sleeping in the sun in your cat bed."

Pandora let out a snore.

I put my hand on her head to feel if she was hot,

and she stirred slightly, purring lazily. "Do I need to take you to the vet?"

Pandora's eyes flew open. *Mewooo.*

Weird, it almost sounded like she said "no" as if she was really trying to communicate with me. It wasn't the first time I'd thought that, but it was the first time I was willing to entertain the thought that it might actually be true.

As soon as I opened the door of my Jeep, my worries about Pandora's health were put to rest. Pandora sprang up and leapt over my lap, out of the car, and onto the porch. I figured the promise of getting her supper must have rejuvenated her.

In the kitchen, Pandora ran straight for her food bowl while I rummaged in the cabinet for cat food. "You want salmon or tuna?"

Meowna.

"Okay, tuna, it is."

I set about filling up her dish, and Pandora hopped up on the counter again, batting at the dandelion tea. This time I didn't yell at her. She was right. I needed to drink some of that tea to encourage an Albert sighting.

"Yeah, I get it. I need to find out about Desmond and Barney." Great, now I was talking to her as if I expected her to understand. Funny thing was, she was looking at me just like she could.

I finished filling her cat bowl and started making tea. Good thing I'd eaten a lot at my late lunch with Striker, because I didn't have any food here. And without Striker to bring me dinner, I'd have to fend for myself.

I found a tomato and a jar of jalapeños in the fridge. I sliced the tomato and set each slice on top of a Triscuit then topped each of those off with a jalapeño ring while the water boiled.

Once everything was ready, I retired to the living room and lounged on the couch, sipping the tea and munching the Triscuits. It was a good combination if not a little spicy. Too bad I didn't have any sour cream to cut the heat.

My gaze fell on the paperweight. Maybe it would show me a clue. But tonight it didn't show anything unless you'd consider a reflection of my white ceiling a clue. Maybe it didn't produce clues on command. It might be like ghosts who never popped up when you wanted information from them but always seemed to be around when you didn't want them.

Across the room, Pandora sat in a chair, staring at me intently. I was glad that she seemed to have perked up, but honestly, it was kind of unnerving the way her unblinking eyes were glued to mine. I stared back, thinking she would look away. Nope, she kept on with her luminescent, unwavering stare. Well, if she thought I was going blink or look away first, she had another think coming.

Out of the corner of my eye, a misty swirl caught my attention, and I wavered.

Meow!

Pandora's triumphant meow indicated her jubilation at winning the staring contest, but I didn't care. The mist was starting to take a human form. I gulped down the rest of the tea.

"Albert?"

The mist continued to materialize. Yep, definitely human.

"Albert, is that you?"

"Huh? Oh, yes, it's me." Albert came into focus.

"How are you doing?" I asked, wondering if that was an appropriate question for a ghost. Albert didn't look like he was doing that great.

"Oh, sorry, Willa. I'm a little distracted. You know the checkers tournament is tomorrow morning, and well... this will be the first time in thirty years that I won't be in it. Seeing all my old friends there..." Albert sighed. "Oh well. Nothing can be done about it, but I feel so very odd."

"I'm sorry, Albert. It must be awful to be in limbo, still seeing your old life but unable to be part of it.

Maybe I can help you move on to the afterlife. I hear it's much nicer than the state you're in now."

Albert perked up. "Oh, really? Well, then I'm all for that." Then he turned thoughtful. "Though I will miss seeing my family."

"I hear over in the afterlife, it only seems like a short while before you are reunited with your loved ones."

Albert looked dismayed. "Well, I wouldn't want them to die soon."

"Oh, no. No," I corrected. "They live out their full lives here, but it just *seems* quick to you over there." At least that was what I'd heard from Franklin and Robert.

Albert appeared to be mollified by that, and he sat down on the chair. "Very well, then. What can I do to help?"

"A couple of things. First I wanted to ask about Barney Delaney. Your son-in-law, Desmond, said he saw you arguing. What did you argue about?"

Albert waved his ghostly hand around. "Oh, that Barney. He's very serious. Guy can't take a joke. You know we both collect stamps, right? Of course, being former postmasters, that's not unusual, and Barney is in the antique business, so he knows a lot. Anyway, he wanted to know if I had any uncanceled stamps from my day. Well, I thought he was implying that I would have stolen them right off the letters! I got a little hotheaded, and we had a row."

"Oh? Why would he think that?"

"Turns out he didn't. It was a misunderstanding. He wasn't implying any such thing. Then, of course, when the talk turned to checkers, it got a little heated again. You know there's a strategy to checkers, and we differ on best practices. It looked like we were arguing, but it was really just passionate debate."

"No, I didn't actually know that," I said, taking another Triscuit, tomato, and jalapeño snack and munching on it. If he and Barney weren't really arguing, then Barney had less of a motive for killing him. This was good information as far as narrowing down suspects went, but I hoped he wasn't going to launch into a long-winded description of how to play checkers. I doubted there was much of a strategy.

Albert scooted forward in his seat. "Oh certainly. Well, you know, if you're the one to go first, you should—"

"Albert," I cut him off. I didn't really have time for this. Ghosts were notorious for not hanging around very long, and I didn't want to waste time talking about checkers when I could be getting the scoop on the next suspect: his son-in-law, Desmond. "I really could use your help on something else."

Albert looked cross. "Well, I thought you said you wanted to hear about checkers strategy."

"Maybe later. First, I want to help you get to the great beyond, and for that, I need to ask about your son-in-law, Desmond. I've heard some talk that he's not quite on the up-and-up."

Albert made a face. "Well, I have to admit, at first, I didn't think he was good enough for my Gemma, but you know, he's not such a bad guy."

"Oh really? You mean you got along well with him?"

"Well, of course we had a few tiffs," Albert scoffed. "But he ended up being okay."

"I heard he was selling off some of your old post-master memorabilia. Stamps and stuff."

"Well, I had given him a few things." Albert's face fell. "I'd hoped he was starting his own collection, but if he was selling them off, I guess not."

"What about his carpal tunnel problem?"

"Yes. Bad thing, that. He's been out of work for quite a while, you know."

"I know, but do you think the problem is real?"

"What? Well, of course it is. The doctor said so."

I sat back and ate another Triscuit. I wondered

about that. Albert seemed pretty sure that Desmond wasn't a faker or a cheater, and I had to admit that I was kind of hoping for Albert's sake that he was right. It would crush him to discover his own son-in-law had killed him.

Albert had said he'd given the stamps and other memorabilia to Desmond, so maybe he hadn't stolen the things he was trying to sell to Barney. It was also possible Albert had given him *some* stamps and memorabilia and Desmond had *taken* some too. I'd have to investigate further. It was clear I wasn't going to get any more information on Desmond from Albert. I had one last person to ask about.

"And what about Nathan Anderson?"

"Who?"

"He's friends with Desmond. Did you ever give him stamps?"

"No. Never heard of him."

That didn't mean much. If Nathan was into something with Desmond or trying to get at the letter through Desmond, Albert wouldn't necessarily know who he was.

"So will you be at the checkers game tomorrow?" I asked.

Albert stood, his ghost swirling and fading. "Of course I will. In spirit. Now I hear the ethers calling. I hope what I had to say was of use, Willa, because this limbo just is not fun. Hopefully you'll be able to help me soon."

Albert poofed away, and I was left in the room, alone with Pandora.

Meow. Pandora looked at me knowingly.

"That wasn't very enlightening, was it?" I asked.

Meoooo.

"But I kind of believed what he said about Desmond, didn't you?"

Pandora trotted over to the couch and jumped up in my lap, rubbing her head against my hand and purring. I took that as agreement. She kind of believed Albert too.

"And it seems like Barney and Albert really were friends. At least they didn't have a big heated disagreement that would warrant Barney killing him."

Meroop.

"I suppose that leaves Felicity," I said.

Pandora stopped purring and jerked her head to look at me. *Meooo.*

I got a very negative vibe from the cat. Clearly, Pandora did not like Felicity. Who could blame her?

"Yeah. I don't like her very much either, and that's why she's my next best suspect. Well, her and Nathan."

Pandora frowned at me. *Maroo.*

Pandora's meow sounded like the word no. As in "No, I don't like her either." No surprise there. I had a feeling she liked Fluff even less, judging by the way they hissed at each other through my store window.

"I really hope Desmond wasn't taking advantage of Albert. Albert seems nice, and I'd hate to think of anyone taking advantage of him like that."

Meow.

"But *someone* killed him. That person's going to have to go to jail. If it turned out to be Felicity, that would just be dandy."

Meyoooow!

I took that as agreement, even though it still sounded like a no.

My phone dinged on the coffee table. A text from Striker.

Thinking of you. Have a good sleep.

Good feelings washed over me as I snuggled down on the couch with Pandora. Albert had cleared up a few things, and I was one step closer to finding his killer. Not only that, but I felt like I was developing a closer bond with my cat, not to mention taking my relationship with Striker to a whole new level.

21

The next morning, I arrived at the bookstore to find the regulars waiting outside with coffees in hand. I unlocked the antique oak door, and Bing handed me a coffee as they made their way to the sofa and chairs.

Pandora trotted over to the seating area and plopped down at Bing's feet then stared up at him adoringly. She never looked at *me* that way.

Josiah sat slumped in his chair, leaning forward, elbows on knees, fiddling with the tab of the Styrofoam cup in his hands.

"What's the matter, Josiah? You look down in the dumps," Bing said.

"Uh, it's nothing, really. The checkers tournament

was this morning, and it just didn't seem right with what happened to Albert."

"Oh dear, I forgot all about that. You guys sure do play early," Hattie said. Today, she was wearing a lavender-colored pantsuit with a white shirt. Cordelia had on a white pantsuit with a lavender-colored shirt. They were both bright-eyed and alert, as usual. Worry washed over me. If the story of the pleasantry charm was true, and it somehow got reversed, how would that affect my regulars? Or me, for that matter.

"It's the postmaster way, you know, getting up early to deliver the mail, so we always hold the checkers tournament at six a.m. Barney won this year, but even he didn't seem that happy about it."

"I could understand, considering the circumstances," Hattie clucked.

"I came in second, but I couldn't take any joy in it." Josiah leaned back and sighed. "Funny thing. The whole time, I felt Albert was there, looking over our shoulders."

I raised a brow but didn't say anything. Little did he know, Albert really was there, looking over their shoulders.

"What's going on with the murder investigation, Willa?" Hattie asked. "Does Gus have any suspects?"

"You know Gus. She doesn't discuss her cases with me," I said.

Cordelia leaned forward and patted me on the knee, her eyes full of mischief. "Yes, but that hunky Sheriff Striker shares things with you now, doesn't he?"

My cheeks warmed, and I sipped my coffee to cover up. "He's not really allowed to tell me about cases or anything."

Cordelia and Hattie exchanged a knowing look. Hattie said, "I'm sure he's not allowed, but I bet he does. Anyway, I think it's probably the son-in-law."

I seized my opportunity. "Didn't you say that your niece knew him or something? What's her name? Brenda?" I actually didn't know their niece's name, but this was a good way to find out.

"Not Brenda, she's the florist. Elise is the nurse." Hattie pressed her lips together. "But she doesn't *know* Desmond. She works at the clinic where he's being treated for that injury."

"Oh, that's right. Is that the clinic on High Street?"

"Yes, it is. Very nice place, and do you know she has her LNA? She went to school for several years for that and..."

I sipped my coffee and let their conversation fade into the background as it turned from Hattie and

Cordelia's niece's resume to the local gossip. I nodded at the appropriate junctures in the conversation, but in my head, I was working a plan.

Maybe I could make use of the charmed truth tea Pepper had mentioned to find out if Desmond really was faking his injury. I knew Striker said Desmond had an alibi for the time of Albert's murder, but what if somehow he faked that too?

For Albert's sake, I hoped the rumors about Desmond were exaggerated, but I was going to find out one way or the other. And by nighttime, I could either cross him off my suspect list or report to Striker that he'd faked the alibi.

As the regulars got up and left, tossing their Styrofoam cups in the trash, I whipped out my phone and texted Pepper.

Meet at 3. We're going to the clinic to find out what Desmond was really up to. Bring your truth tea.

She texted back right away.

Count me in.

I had the rest of the day to wait, so I started shelving books. Hanna had the day off. I could've left the stocking for her to do tomorrow, but I liked staying busy. Pandora was zonked out in the cat bed again, but I got the impression, even though she was sleeping, she was watching me. It seemed like she was waiting for something. Probably worried I was going to make good on my threat to bring her to the vet.

I spent the rest of the morning stocking the bookshelves and waiting on customers. I had a pretty good day, selling several old Agatha Christie hardcovers and some newer paperbacks from some of my favorite mystery authors.

Shortly after noon, the bells chimed, and Striker came in.

He smiled upon seeing me, and I felt we'd turned a corner in our relationship. Things were different now, and it was for the better. Now we shared a secret, and it was bringing us closer.

"Hey, I just wanted to swing by." He glanced down the aisles to see if anyone else was in the store. "Seen any ghosts lately?"

"Well, as a matter of fact, I did talk to Albert last night." I picked up some history books and gestured for him to follow me down to the history aisle.

"And what did he have to say? Anything enlightening?"

"He seems to think Desmond is on the up-and-up."

Striker made a face. "He was on Gus's suspect list but came up with an alibi, like I told you yesterday. You still think he faked it?"

"Maybe. I wanted to double-check with Albert," I said, shoving a book into its spot on the shelf. "It's always good to double-check things. People lie. I also found out that Albert and Barney Delaney had somewhat of an adversarial friendship but nothing one would kill over, according to Albert."

"Okay, Gus has Delaney on her suspect list too."

"How are things going with Gus, anyway? Are you able to steer her in the direction we want?"

"No steering necessary. Really, we just want to find the killer, right? We don't need magic or ghosts for that, just good old-fashioned detective work. 'Course, if we get a good tip from a spirit, I'm all for following that up too. Either way, we put the killer behind bars, and if there is any truth to this pleasantry charm and the ingredients, then we won't have to worry, because the killer won't be free to dig it up."

"Yeah, I suppose so." I couldn't help but wonder what was going to happen if we didn't find the letter. Would it fall into evil hands? Somehow I knew instinctively that we had to make sure the letter was safe, but how? Only one way: we had to catch the killer *with* the letter. Or search their house for it after they were caught.

Striker stepped closer, his finger tracing a line on

the back of my hand. "Don't worry. We'll catch the person and get the letter."

Had he read my thoughts?

"No, he can't read thoughts." Franklin popped up beside Striker, scaring the bejesus out of me.

Striker looked concerned. "What is it?"

"You can't see him?" I gestured to where Franklin stood, and Striker looked.

"No, I don't see anyone."

Robert Frost popped up next to Franklin. "He can't see us. Only you can. Didn't we mention that?"

Franklin nodded. "Your grandmother put us in place to protect the store, and as the new owner, you get to be the only human to see us. Aren't you lucky?"

"Yeah, real lucky."

"Yeah, we are lucky," Striker said, then his frown deepened. "Wait. Is there some ghost here that I can't see?"

I nodded. I didn't really want to tell him that the ghosts were Franklin Pierce and Robert Frost. That was stretching it a little too far. Maybe once we knew each other a lot better. "Two, actually. Bookstore ghosts. They just stay in the store, apparently."

Striker looked around as if wishing he could see them. He waved his hand through the air right at Franklin's midsection. Franklin doubled over in mock pain just as Striker pulled his hand back. "I do feel something cold."

"Yep, that was one of them."

"Huh. Kinda neat. Well, I guess I can't see them all."

"Hopefully, you can see the important ones, though."

"Yeah, hopefully. Between the two of us, I think we have the spirit world covered." Striker stepped closer. "I don't see anyone in the shop, so seeing as we're alone..."

I glanced behind him to see Franklin and Robert tittering. If you've never seen ghosts titter, it's something to behold. They looked rather silly with their shoulders touching and hands over their mouths as their ghostly figures swirled around. Robert raised his bushy white eyebrows and nodded at me then pointed to Striker. "He's a keeper." And then the two of them disappeared.

"We are now."

Striker leaned forward and planted a soft kiss on my lips. It was sweet and gentle and tasted like tuna fish sandwiches. Okay, maybe the tuna part wasn't so pleasant, but the rest of it was.

"I'm glad that we have this new connection," he said.

"Me too."

He stepped away, and I resisted the urge to pull him back.

"But I don't want you to think that our new connection means I'm going to look the other way while you put yourself in danger."

Uh-oh. Here it came. Now he would start acting like Gus.

"Okay," I said with a noncommittal tone.

"Seriously, I don't want you doing anything crazy. There's a dangerous killer around, and who knows what kinds of things he can do? If it's someone that knows about magic, or a so-called witch like Felicity, they could fight back in unexpected ways. And while I appreciate your help, I think you really should leave the detecting up to the cops."

"Oh, I will. I'm just gathering information for you," I said.

He backed away down the aisle. "Okay, but I want you to promise not to take any dangerous chances."

I smiled and nodded. "I promise."

Striker left, and I stared after him as he disappeared down the aisle, wondering if it was a bad thing that I hadn't told him about my upcoming excursion with Pepper. Going to the clinic and asking about Desmond wouldn't be dangerous, would it?

I proceeded to stock books and tidy up the shop, keeping an eye on a sleepy Pandora until Pepper arrived promptly at three. To my dismay, she did not have her quilted tea cozy.

"What's going on? I thought you were going to bring a tea to help make Hattie's niece talk?"

"Oh, I did." She held up an insulated travel mug with her shop logo on it. "It's in here. I didn't think it would be normal to bring a whole tea cozy to the clinic. That only makes sense when you are visiting someone at their home, so I opted for just putting it in this mug. It should stay warm until we get there."

Oh, good idea. I grabbed a couple of coupons from my counter. "I'm going to pretend like I'm there to give her a coupon as part of a friends-and-family promotion. Since Hattie and Cordelia are such good friends, I wanted to swing by with the coupon for Elise."

"Good thinking." Pepper had gone over to Pandora's cat bed and was stroking her and murmuring like you would to a child. Pandora looked up at her. The sun filtering through the window gave her eyes a golden glow as she meowed softly at my friend.

"I think she might not be feeling well," I said.

Pepper frowned at me. "No, she's fine. Just tired."

"Tired? From what?"

Pepper smiled and glanced at Pandora. "Cat stuff. You know."

I didn't know, but I also didn't have time to wonder about it. I was on a mission. "Are you ready to go?"

Pepper stopped petting and came over to the door. "Yep."

I opened the door and gestured for her to go out first so I could lock it up. She turned back to Pandora and gave a little wave. "You be good now, you hear?"

Meow!

I wasn't sure what the meow meant, but somehow I doubted Pandora was agreeing to "be good."

22

Pandora watched Willa and Pepper get into Willa's Jeep. Finally! She'd thought Willa would never leave. Her seventh sense had told her hours ago that the cats were on the scent of Nathan Anderson, and she didn't want to miss out.

Pandora ran for the closet and made her escape, glancing back down the street to see Barney Delaney at the front door of the bookshop. Oh well, he wasn't going to get in for another free reference book. Yeah, Pandora had been keeping track, and Barney still owed Willa money.

She watched as he cupped his hands to his face and looked in the narrow window beside the oak door then peered into the front window. Finally, he noticed the closed sign and proceeded to take a blue Post-it note pad out of his pocket, write a note, and stick it on the window. Who carried Post-it note pads with them?

Maybe he was going to make good on that book, though. That would be good. Willa needed to watch finances to keep Pandora supplied with the premium cat food she favored. Speaking of Willa, Pandora was getting a little frustrated with the lack of communication. Sure, it seemed like Willa was warming to the idea of communicating with her, but she was getting the transmissions all wrong.

Take all her talk about Felicity Bates last night, for example. Pandora had tried to tell her Felicity was not the killer and that she didn't have the letter, but did Willa listen? No. She thought Pandora was expressing her dislike for Felicity. Granted she liked the redheaded witch about as much as she liked getting a hairball stuck in her throat, but that was totally not what she'd been trying to tell her human.

It made Pandora nervous because she didn't want Willa to focus on Felicity and ignore the real killer. But if that killer was Nathan Anderson and the cats could do something to catch him today, maybe she wouldn't have to worry about Willa's safety much longer.

Pandora turned and raced toward the section of town where her instincts told her the other cats were hunting Nathan. She didn't have a minute to lose.

* * *

The High Street Clinic was shiny and modern. It was fairly new, built in the past few years, and the waiting room was pungent with the scent of rubbing alcohol. We asked for Hattie's niece and were told to wait in the plush waiting room, which was practically empty.

A soap opera played on the wall-mounted large-screen TV, and we waited patiently. Soon, a perky woman in her late thirties, dressed in pink scrubs, came out to greet us.

"Hi, I'm Elise." She held her hand out and looked at us expectantly.

I shook her hand. "I'm Willa Chance, from Last Chance Books. I'm a friend of your aunts, Hattie and Cordelia."

"Oh. They're actually my great aunts. Aren't they a hoot?" Elise said.

"They sure are."

Concern flickered in her brown eyes. "I hope nothing has happened to them."

"Oh no, not at all. I just came by to give you this." I shoved the coupon at her. "I'm running a promotion for friends and family of my favorite customers. Hattie and Cordelia told me how busy you are, and I had an errand nearby, so thought I would drop it off."

She looked down at the coupon. "Why, that's very nice. Thank you."

Her eyes fell on Pepper, and Pepper shoved the travel mug at her. "And I'm Pepper St. Onge. I run The Tea Shoppe downtown, and I brought a special tea to introduce you to my herbal blends."

Elise took the mug and looked at it, apparently not sure what to do with it.

"There's tea in it. It's hot and freshly made. It'll taste the best if you drink it now," Pepper added.

"Okay." Elise took the mug and sipped then smacked her lips together. "Well, it is quite tasty. What is it?"

"It's a blend of herbs and flowers. It's supposed to give you energy for your workday. I figured it would be especially good for you, since you work with a lot of sick people, because it also has medicinal properties that will help bolster your immune system."

I glanced sideways at Pepper. Had she just made that up, or was it really true?

"That sounds perfect." Elise took another big gulp.

I glanced at Pepper again. Was it okay for me to start questioning her? Pepper nodded subtly.

"Have you heard about Albert Schumer, the retired postmaster? I think your aunts knew him."

"Oh, yes. Terrible. Albert was a nice man. He used

to come in for his lipid tests." Elise made a face as if she realized she shouldn't have told us that.

"Right, and his son-in-law, Desmond, came here too for his carpal tunnel."

"Oh, yes. That's right. He did. Dr. Green operated on him. I believe that was about a month ago, but his stitches got infected. Now, you know, I told him to watch out for that. Not to get it wet. Keep it covered. Not to get anything on it and to clean it very carefully because infections can set in easily." Elise covered her mouth with her free hand and glanced at the tea. She hiccuped then added, "In fact, he was right here at the very time Albert died. The police came and asked me about it. I could vouch because I happened to be on duty."

So much for him faking his alibi.

"Are you sure?"

Elsie slurped more of the drink. "Yes, I even double-checked in the system for the police. It's all computerized with the time the patient comes in and so on."

"I'd heard a rumor that he didn't even really need that operation," I said.

"Oh, no. He needed it. His job is very repetitive, and he had a strain in his arm. I know it was quite necessary."

"Really? And you don't think he could work?"

"Oh, no. There's no working for at least eight weeks after it, and he's still not even in his eighth week."

The receptionist slid the glass window open. "Elise, Dr. Martin needs you in room five."

"Oh, gotta go." Elise held up the mug and coupon. "Thanks for stopping by."

She disappeared through a door, and I turned to Pepper. "Will she be okay to work?"

"She'll be fine. The tea wears off quickly." Pepper held the door open for me, and we exited out into the sunshine. "It may cause her to confess to any doctors she has a secret crush on them, though that may not necessarily be a bad thing."

"So I guess Desmond can't be the killer," I said as we got settled in my Jeep.

"Seems like his alibi is airtight if it's tracked in the system, and Elise would have told you the truth." A self-satisfied smile played on Pepper's lips. "Because she drank my tea."

"I'm not sure if I'm happy about that or not." I pulled out of the parking lot and headed back toward our shops. "I'm glad for Albert, but Desmond seemed sketchy. He had dealings with Nathan Anderson, and I saw Nathan with Felicity outside my shop."

"Nathan and Felicity could be in on it together," Pepper said. "Emma told you she saw Nathan driving away from the post office that morning, and we know Felicity isn't exactly one to want positivity in Mystic Notch."

"I also saw Nathan following Barney Delaney... Either that, or he was spying on me."

"Maybe he was spying for Felicity."

"Hmm... Good point. I hadn't thought about that," I said. "Either way, I think I'll warn Barney to be careful. He's a bit of a grouch, but I don't want to see anything happen to him."

"So you don't think he might have killed Albert to win the checkers tournament?" Pepper asked.

I glanced over at her. Was she serious? "That would be kind of drastic, wouldn't it?"

"Yeah, I suppose. Hester's letter is a much more compelling reason for murder, and we don't even know if it had a rare stamp. Desmond might have tried to sell it to Barney, but then it would likely just be the envelope."

"And Barney would have just bought it, not waited around to kill Albert for it," I said. "According to Albert, he gave Desmond post office memorabilia, so that might have been what Desmond tried to sell to

Barney. Desmond probably didn't know a thing about the letter and its magical ramifications."

"Yeah, and Desmond isn't from an old Mystic Notch family, but Nathan and Felicity are," Pepper pointed out as I parked at the curb.

We said our goodbyes and headed toward our individual shops. A quick glance at Pandora's empty cat bed perked me up. The fact that she wasn't lazing around made me feel better about her health. She was probably in back, scheming up some kind of payback for leaving without her.

For once, I might not mind that she'd knocked all my pens on the floor or clawed all the toilet paper off the roll in the bathroom and papered my back hall with it. I wouldn't even mind a hairball under the couch if it meant Pandora was back to her usual perky self.

As I dug out my key, my mind drifted to Felicity. I'd seen her outside the shop, arguing about a letter with Nathan. And why would they be arguing? Only one reason. One of them had it, and the other one wanted it. I mentally crossed Desmond off my list and moved Felicity and Nathan to the top. I really wanted it to be Felicity—and I was sure she wanted the letter—but it was Nathan's car that had been seen fleeing the murder scene.

But then why had Nathan been following Barney? Why wasn't he running around town, digging up the ingredients? Hmm... Maybe not all the ingredients were buried in the earth.

Pepper had said that Hester Warren had buried *and* hidden ingredients. Maybe some of them were hidden in other items. Antique items. Barney had a lot of strange old antiques. Maybe one of the ingredients was right in his shop. But if so, why wouldn't Nathan just buy it? Barney had seemed disgusted with Desmond and Nathan before. Was it possible he'd refused to sell it to Nathan, and Nathan was planning to take it by force? Perhaps use the tools he'd claimed had been stolen from his shed?

Had Nathan been stalking Barney to try to figure out when he could break into his shop and take the item? But he hadn't broken in. If he had, Striker would have told me. He might still be intending to break in, and if he got desperate enough, he might not care whether Barney was there or not. My gut clenched—Barney could be in danger.

As I fished out my key, I noticed a blue Post-it note stuck to the side window. Speak of the devil, it was a note from Barney. He wanted me to stop by his shop to settle up for the book I'd let him take. I was sure he'd still be open.

It was late afternoon, and the street behind me was practically empty. No sign of Nathan Anderson's silver Prius. No sign of Felicity either. That made me feel safer. The promise I'd made to Striker about being careful rang in my ears, but walking to Barney's antique store could hardly be dangerous if Nathan and Felicity were nowhere about.

I cast another glance at the empty cat bed. Maybe it was a good time to pay Barney a visit and collect my money. I could warn him to watch out for Nathan. Hopefully, by the time I got back, Pandora would be done wreaking whatever kind of havoc she had in store for me inside the shop. I shoved the Post-it note in my pocket and headed toward Barney's.

23

Pandora approached the group of cats silently. "He's acting very suspicious," Tigger whispered. "What's he doing?"

Inkspot narrowed his gaze on the human clawing through the dirt with his hands. "Obviously trying to find another ingredient for the spell."

"Well." Otis snorted. "Must not be buried very deep if he doesn't have a shovel."

As if hearing their hushed conversation, Nathan stopped digging and glared over his shoulder in their direction. All five cats hunched back into the shadows. Pandora's mind raced. Had he heard them? No, it was impossible. Unless a feline chose to reveal themselves to a human and formed a telepathic connection with them, their quiet murmurs would only sound like whispers of wind to humans.

"This one is different. I am sure he is up to something," Kelley said.

Nathan straightened slightly, brushing his hands against the legs of his jeans. Then his gaze locked on Kelley, and he strode toward them, his expression furious.

Panic surged through Pandora.

Inkspot hissed loudly, baring his teeth. "Attack!"

The cats charged Nathan, claws sharp as they leapt onto his legs and arms. Nathan stopped in his tracks, yelping as he was scratched and bitten. "Wait! Hold on!"

Pandora, who'd dug her claws into Nathan's thigh, noticed the hands he held up in surrender in front of her. No scratches. Kelley had said the killer had cut themselves on the glass container of the first ingredient. A sinking feeling bubbled up inside her. This might very well be a mistake.

"Please stop!" Nathan pleaded. "You'll ruin everything."

Inkspot leaned back from where he was hanging off Nathan's arm and stared into the man's eyes. "Are you speaking to us?" he said telepathically.

"Yes," Nathan said, his tone low. "Do you see anyone else around?"

"But we're cats." Otis slowly retracted his claws from Nathan's ankle. "No one talks to cats."

Nathan exhaled slowly then crouched down to allow the rest of the felines to climb off of him. “Some of us do.”

All the cats exchanged a look then convened off to the side of the clearing to discuss the situation.

“How is this possible?” Pandora asked.

“I’ve heard stories of a rare lineage descended from Hester Warren who can actually speak to cats,” Tigger said. “It is rumored Hester spoke to her cat, Obsidian. Maybe Nathan is one of them.”

“If that’s the case, then why is he trying to dig up the ingredients?” Inkspot asked, his words laced with suspicion. “Makes no sense to me.”

“He doesn’t have any scratches.” Kelley sniffed in Nathan’s direction. “I cannot make out his blood type, but whoever dug up the first ingredient was cut. I am sure of it.”

Otis narrowed his eyes in Nathan’s direction. “Then there are two perpetrators. This one is most dangerous.”

“I can hear you, you know,” Nathan said.

“Tell us why you killed Albert Schumer and where you hid the letter,” Inkspot demanded.

“Listen, I swear I’m not Albert’s killer,” Nathan said, walking over to join them. “I know about the letter, though. My grandmother told me about the list a long time ago. Our family is sworn to protect it. So, when Desmond mentioned Albert finding an old, undelivered letter from

Hester Warren, I suspected that's what it was. But I give you my magical oath that I did not kill Albert Schumer. I did, however, follow him that day that he went to the post office to make sure he made it there safely to mail the letter. Turns out I was too late. He was already dead when I arrived, and the letter was gone."

"Why should we believe you?" Hope asked.

Nathan frowned. "I... well... I' m not sure." He paused for a minute then rolled up his sleeves. "Look, you said whoever has been digging the ingredients up was cut. I don't have any cuts."

The cats craned their necks forward. It was true, not a scratch on him.

They exchanged a glance, their eyes luminescent slits in the darkening twilight.

"If he is working with someone else, then the other person could have dug up the first ingredient," Otis said. "Pandora's human was told Nathan was seen fleeing the scene of the crime."

Nathan frowned. 'What? Oh no! I can explain."

"Can you also explain why you were arguing with Felicity Bates outside the bookstore? Perhaps you are working with her," Pandora said. They already knew Felicity didn't have the letter, though. And if she didn't have it and wasn't the one who dug up the ingredient in the glass

container, then she couldn't be the one working with Nathan.

"I'm not working with *Felicity Bates." Nathan sounded disgusted. "She's descended from the evil side. Oh, sure, I pretend to get along with her, but that's only to keep an eye on her."*

Hope cocked her head to study Nathan. Pandora could see her skepticism was diminishing. She was starting to believe Nathan, and so was Pandora. "You did say they were arguing, Pandora. He may be telling the truth."

Nathan nodded eagerly. Encouraged that someone believed him, he rushed on with his explanation. "Of course she knew the letter had surfaced. She tried to bribe me into getting it for her, but until Desmond mentioned Albert having it, I had no idea how to find the letter."

"So Desmond knew the importance of the letter?" Pandora asked. Could it have been Desmond all along? He had an alibi for the murder, but if he was working with someone else...

"He said he thought the envelope contained a valuable stamp. He even tried to sell it to Barney Delaney, but Barney turned him down." Nathan looked off into the distance. "In fact, Barney wouldn't buy anything from Desmond, so I pretended like I wanted to work with him, selling stamps and post office memorabilia, so he would hand over the letter. But by that time, it was too late. Albert

had already noticed the letter had never been delivered and was determined to bring it to the post office."

"And that's why you followed him," Inkspot said.

"Yes. To make sure the letter got mailed, like I said. The recipient, my great-aunt, is long gone, but my family still lives in the house, so I just needed to make sure the letter got delivered, and it would be safe."

"Then you must have seen the killer," Sasha pointed out.

Nathan's face fell. "No, unfortunately, I stayed far behind Albert because I didn't want him to see me following. I knew he was going to the post office, so I waited about ten minutes. But when I got there, Albert was dead, and the letter and the killer were both gone."

Pandora's whiskers twitched. "But how is that possible? You would have seen the car at least."

"You'd think, but I didn't see any car."

"The killer must have been on foot," Tigger said. "He or she escaped through the dense shrubbery at the edge of the parking lot onto the side street."

Sasha nodded. "They could have parked on any of the side streets."

Inkspot trotted over to the place where Nathan had been digging and sniffed at the disturbed earth. "Nothing magic was buried here. Why were you digging?"

"And why use your hands?" Kelley added.

Nathan looked down at his dirty hands. "It's the weirdest thing. Someone broke into my toolshed and stole my shovel, so I have nothing to dig with. I assume whoever it is is trying to frame me."

"But what made you come here to this spot?" Inkspot persisted.

"I've narrowed down the list of people who could be interested in the letter to two. I've been following them around. I want to protect the letter, and now that I think I'm being framed, I need to make sure the killer is apprehended. I followed one of my suspects here and thought she might have been digging up one of the relics. She didn't walk away with anything, though, so I hoped she'd dug in the wrong place, and I thought I'd try to recover the ingredient myself."

Inkspot's eyes narrowed. "She?"

"Felicity Bates. From what you said earlier, it sounds like you suspect her too."

Inkspot's tail twitched. "We did, but it can't be her. We've determined she does not have the letter or the first ingredient."

"You have? But..." Nathan frowned. "Oh dear... Yes, now it makes perfect sense."

"It does?" Otis asked.

"Yes, it couldn't be Felicity, so it must be my other suspect."

"And who is that?" Inkspot asked.

"Why it could only be one person," Nathan said. "The antique shop owner, Barney Delaney."

The hairs on Pandora's spine stood on end as her blood chilled. The last thing she had seen as she trotted away from the bookstore was Barney leaving the note for Willa. If Barney was the killer and he knew Willa had been asking around, then she could be in grave danger!

24

Barney was waiting for me when I arrived at his shop. He opened the door for me and escorted me inside to where he'd been inspecting some coins.

"I was just about to close up. Excuse me while I finish grading these coins." He slipped behind the counter where he had a self-standing lighted magnifying glass, slipped on a pair of white cotton archivist gloves, and picked up a small silver coin.

He squinted into the magnifying glass. "Oh yes... this one looks to be in EF condition." He looked up over the rim of the magnifier at me. "That means 'extra fine.' Not the best but will bring a tidy sum." He snapped off the light and placed the coin in a plastic sleeve.

"So, settling up for that book then," I said to get

things moving along lest the man make me suffer through more coin grading. I wanted to warn Barney about Nathan, but I didn't know quite exactly how to put it.

As he fiddled around behind the desk, I did my best to remain polite and forced a smile I didn't quite feel. For some odd reason, Barney seemed nervous—barely meeting my gaze since I'd arrived. He futzed around with some items on the counter while I did my best to put him at ease. "You really don't have to—"

"That wasn't the reason I asked you here," he said, cutting me off. "Not really."

Barney raked a hand through his thinning white hair and exhaled slowly. "Honestly, I debated long and hard if I should even mention this to you, Willa. I don't want to get anyone in trouble, see, and I don't like stirring up issues when there are none, but Nathan brought this into my store earlier because he wanted an appraisal on the stamp." He held out a yellowed envelope. "After he left, I got to thinking this might be the letter Albert was trying to mail. It's not postmarked."

I took it from him, doing my best not to tremble as I spied the return address—Helen Warren. Oh no. I knew it! Nathan was the killer. And my assumption about him following Barney was right. But the envelope was empty. Where was the letter?

"Like I said, Nathan dropped it off to see if the stamp on it had any value." Barney turned away. "I haven't had a chance to do much research into it yet."

"Is there anything inside the envelope?" I asked, my voice sounding strained, even to my own ears.

"Nope. Nothing."

My heart sank even as my mind whirled. It made sense. If Nathan discovered the letter listing the ingredients and their locations to lift the pleasantry charm, then he wouldn't need the envelope. He could get money for the stamp if it was rare and still have the letter.

Barney walked behind the counter and opened his cash register drawer, withdrawing the money for the coin book he'd taken from my shop. He handed it to me, and I pocketed the money before handing him back the envelope.

"Thanks," I said, heading for the exit and eager to call Striker to tell him what had happened. "You might want to be careful around Nathan."

"Oh dear, really?" Barney said from behind me, forcing me to stop. When had he slipped out from behind the counter? "I thought I saw Nathan a little bit ago, out in the woods behind the shop here. It's nearly dark now, and I've not seen his Prius again. Why would he want to go out in the woods at night?"

To dig up more ingredients.

I didn't say that out loud, though. Barney didn't know anything about the pleasantry charm or the list of ingredients. As near as I could tell, the majority of Mystic Notch residents had no idea what went on behind the scenes here in town. Instead, I fished for more information, thinking that perhaps tonight might be the perfect time to catch a killer.

"Huh," I said, trying to look only mildly concerned even though my heart was threatening to pound out of my chest with all the adrenaline pumping through my system. "So, you think he's still out there?"

"Think so, yeah." Barney frowned at me. "You aren't planning on going out there, are you, Willa? That's not wise, and I won't hear of it. Not alone. If you want to see where he went, then I'm coming with you. It'll be easier to show you rather than tell you."

The bells of First Hope Church were chiming six times for six p.m. as Barney locked the front door and led me around to the back door of his shop, which opened into a dense part of the town forest.

Wind gusted, and leaves crackled around our feet as we walked into the trees. The zing of adrenaline in my bloodstream soon burned away, leaving a gnawing path of dark unease in its wake. It might have been smarter to call Striker instead of coming out here with only Barney to protect me. The promise I'd made about not doing anything dangerous echoed in my head. I could call him now, but then I'd really be in trouble. Better to just see what was going on out here first.

But the farther we went, the uneasier I became. Night had fallen, and with it, so had the temperature. I hunkered down inside my jacket and clenched my hands in my pockets to keep them from shaking.

Every noise seemed ominous. The crackle of branches, the whisper of unseen creatures stirring, the chill of coming winter in the air. My overactive imagination went wild, streaming facts about Albert's case.

Emma Potts claimed she'd seen Nathan driving past the church parking lot as the church bells had chimed six in the morning. But Striker had told me the ME had confirmed Albert Schumer's time of death at five forty-five. That was fifteen minutes before Emma had seen Nathan's Prius. Surely it wouldn't take Nathan fifteen minutes to find Albert's letter when he'd been carrying it in his hand, right? Seemed more logical that he'd bash Albert on the head, take the letter, and get the heck out of there to avoid discovery.

So why had Nathan hung around so long at the scene of the crime?

I stumbled on uneven ground and grabbed Barney's arm to steady myself. I noticed he still had on his white gloves from the store. As I looked down, one of the gloves slipped down on his hand, and I saw a long scratch.

It was then that I realized I'd made the worst mistake of my life.

25

"Willa may be with Barney Delaney right now," Pandora said, her panic rising by the second. "I saw him leave a note for her as I left to come here."

"I know Willa's been investigating the murder and checking into suspects like Barney. And if I know that, then so does he." Nathan's expression turned deadly serious as he peered into the dense forest. "We need to find them. Someone broke into my toolshed earlier today and stole the shovel. If that was Barney, he could be preparing to put Willa into a shallow grave."

"No!" Pandora hissed loudly, all her nerves on high alert. "I must save her!"

"I'll take you in my car." Nathan started toward the road.

"No." Inkspot stopped him. "We can run faster through the woods."

Inkspot started toward town, but Pandora hesitated. What if Barney had a gun? What good would a bunch of cats be against that? No... she needed human help.

"You guys keep him from hurting Willa. I'm going for help!" Pandora yelled as the others followed Inkspot.

"Wait!" Otis sprinted after her through the trees, surprisingly agile despite his extra bulk. He cut Pandora off and forced her to stop. "Where are you going?"

"To get Striker."

"And how are you going to tell him what's wrong?" Otis gave her a flat stare. "I know you said you've been making headway, but—"

"I'll do it. Don't worry." Pandora lifted her head high. "I know you don't believe me, but tonight I'm going to put my money where my meow is. I'm going to break through the telepathic barrier holding Striker back from communicating with me. Now, if you'll excuse me, I need to get to the police station immediately!"

"Okay, but be careful, and may Bastet be with you!"

Otis's words were only slight comfort as she took off toward the Mystic Notch Police Station. She only hoped she could make good on her confident prediction about communicating with Striker.

26

The Mystic Notch Police Station was quiet when Pandora arrived. She'd sprinted all the way over and had to take a moment to catch her breath. Luckily, one of the deputies left shortly after she got there, allowing her to slip through the open door inside the place.

She'd only been there a few times before, so it took a bit of time to get acclimated and remember where exactly Striker was. Once located, she stalked over and prepared to jump up onto the desk he was using while he finished up a phone call.

"Yes, Ms. Charles. I realize you think the rose bush in your front yard is haunted, but please remember it's a windy night and some of those noises are natural." He winced and held the phone away from his ear, turning

away. That was when he spotted Pandora. A frown creased his brow.

Striker finished up the conversation with Ms. Charles by assuring her he'd swing by in his squad car later then hung up the phone. Pandora leapt onto his desktop and took a seat in front of him, atop a stack of paperwork, tail swishing and eyes intent on his.

"How'd you get in?" Striker asked before looking around the room. "Is Willa with you?"

No, Willa wasn't with her. That was the problem. Pandora took a deep breath then focused all her concentration on the human male before her, compelling his attention back to her.

He craned his neck to see around her, clearly expecting Willa to appear in his doorway. "Okay, where is she? And why in the world would she bring you here?"

"Hey, why wouldn't she?" Pandora bristled.

Oh dear, Striker didn't seem to be receiving her telepathic thoughts. He kept petting her and looking for Willa. Pandora stared at him and focused harder.

Striker leaned forward slightly, his gray gaze narrowing, his pupils dilating slightly. "What is it, girl? What's wrong?"

The air between them seemed to sizzle, and Pandora felt the barrier between her mind and his waver then disappear completely. She was in!

Pandora began to send messages of panic and warning. Willa in trouble! Willa need help!

In return, she could feel his concern for her human caretaker, his razor-sharp intelligence, and his kind, brave heart. That was good. They'd need those qualities to save Willa from danger tonight.

"Willa's in danger," Striker whispered, speaking in time to Pandora's thoughts. "Willa needs my help." He blinked then jumped to his feet. "Willa's in danger! Willa needs my help."

Without asking, he scooped Pandora up under one arm and jammed his hat on his head before grabbing his car keys and badge from the desktop. "Where is she, girl? Tell me where to go."

Normally, Pandora would have hissed, clawed, and squirmed to get away. Being carried under someone's arm was so undignified. But these were special circumstances, and causing a ruckus would only delay them getting to Willa. Instead, she sent telepathic images of Barney's antique store and the woods behind it as they headed for the squad car. After he set Pandora in the passenger seat, Striker climbed in behind the wheel and started the engine, giving a bark of disbelieving laughter. "It's a good thing Gus isn't around," he said. "Otherwise, I'd have some explaining to do about why I'm driving around Mystic Notch with her sister's cat."

Pandora answered with an urgent meow that had Striker squealing out of the station parking lot in a blaze of rubber and flashing lights.

"Right," Striker said, frowning. "Doesn't matter now. All that matters is making sure Willa is safe."

They pulled up outside the store moments later, and Striker got out let Pandora out the passenger side. "Where to now? Are they inside or out here somewhere?"

Pandora took a moment to get her bearings. Her whiskers twitched, her nose high in the air, seeking the scent of Willa. She wasn't inside the antique shop. She was beyond it in the woods. This was not good.

Pandora rushed around the side of the building toward the woods. Behind her, she heard Striker's muttered curse then the pounding of his footsteps as he followed behind her into the darkness.

"Guess it's the woods, then," he said, his tone dry.

27

I swallowed hard, staring down the barrel of Barney Delaney's gun and resisting the urge to kick myself for not noticing before now that he had a weapon under his coat. Gus was right. I should leave the murder investigations to trained professionals like her.

"Keep moving," he growled, waving the weapon in front of my face. "Can't stop now."

"Barney, why are you doing this?" I asked, futilely stalling for time. No one was coming to help me. I knew that. I'd foolishly wandered off without telling anyone where I was going. Even Pandora didn't know where I'd gone.

My chest constricted at the thought of her back in the bookstore, wondering when I would come back.

Maybe never. I hoped someone would figure out she was in there and feed her. Who would take care of her? Wait, it wasn't productive to think like that. I'd gotten myself out of much worse predicaments. Okay, maybe not worse but at least just as bad. I needed to keep Barney talking until I could figure a way out of this mess. "It's not too late."

"You're wrong." He shook his head. "It was too late from the minute I saw you hesitate when those bells rang at the church. You know what happened, and now I need to take care of it. Now get walking."

He was nothing if not perceptive. Yes, I'd figured it out from the bells. Barney must have hidden his car on the side street and walked over to the post office, killed Albert, then rushed to the diner to establish his alibi. Score one for me, amateur detective. Too bad I hadn't figured it out about a half hour sooner.

He gestured with the gun, and I plodded forward through the trees, wet mud and leaves sucking at my shoes. I continued to press for answers. "You never answered my question, Barney. Why do this? Why did you kill Albert?"

Silence reigned for so long I thought he wouldn't answer. Then he spoke in quiet tones, so low I wouldn't have heard him if I'd not been paying attention.

"I'm a descendent of Miles Danforth, one of the original magical families that settled here in Mystic Notch," he said. "I knew about the pleasantry charm and the buried ingredients well before that letter surfaced. In fact, I've already collected the first one and have it hidden amongst the items in my shop."

Guess that explained the weird vibes I got in there.

"Don't bother looking for it though," he continued. "No one will ever find it."

"So, you plan to gather the rest of the ingredients and lift the charm. Why?"

"Because it's time for a little shake-up around town. Things have been too peaceful for too long. Mystic Notch has become nothing but a quaint little tourist trap, full of tacky souvenirs and cheap T-shirts. That's never what the founders of the town intended. Never."

"And you think creating chaos will help?" I did my best to keep the censure from my tone and failed miserably, if the glare Barney gave me as we walked was any indication. "Seems like it would only hurt a lot of people."

"Maybe some will be hurt, but others like me will be helped."

We stopped in a small clearing near a babbling brook. As I scanned the area, I spotted a shovel leaning against the trunk of a tree, and my heart sank.

"I'm sorry it has come to this, Willa." Barney might have been sorry but not enough to prevent him from jamming his gun in my back hard enough to make me yelp as he guided me toward the tree with the shovel. "But you were too nosy for your own good."

"What are you going to do?" I considered running, but given my bad leg and the darkness and the fact that he had a loaded gun handy, my chances didn't seem good. "Kill me?"

"As a matter of fact, yeah. Got a brilliant plan all worked out, actually." Barney sounded proud of himself. I wanted to kick him hard in the shins. "See that shovel there? I'm going to conk you on the head with it then shove your body in the stream there. You float off, trace evidence gets washed away, and I escape, then I can come back later and blame it all on Nathan Anderson since the shovel belongs to him."

"You're the one who broke into his shed earlier, aren't you?" I wasn't always the brightest bulb in the lamp, but I had my moments. "And that's why you're wearing the gloves tonight, huh? No fingerprints."

"Bingo." Barney's teeth shone dull white in the moonlight. "Since you've been sticking your nose into Nathan's business too, following him around and all, you just made my job a lot easier. The cops already suspect him of Albert's murder, seeing as how he was at the scene of Albert's death. Yeah, I saw him pull up just as I was slipping through those shrubs. Figure all I need to do is tell Gus that Nathan tried to sell me that stamp on the envelope, and she'll take care of the rest. After all, she's got no clue about the true value of that letter, and that dummy Desmond Lacroix can verify he told Nathan his father-in-law had the envelope."

I did my best to stay calm and not panic, though adrenaline pounded through my system like a jackhammer. "Where's the letter now?"

"Right here." Barney pulled it from his pocket with his free hand and waved it in the air. "Once I finish getting all the ingredients, Mystic Notch will be restored to the great town my ancestors intended it to be."

I watched as he waved the letter. If nothing else, maybe I could somehow destroy it. But the gun was still pointing at me. To lunge for it would be a death sentence. I had to think of something quickly.

"And now it's time for you to die." Barney lowered his hand, about to put the letter back in his pocket.

I tensed. It was now or never. He was old. Maybe I could overpower him.

Meroowww!

A god-awful screech echoed through the air, followed by a white ball of flying fur.

I ducked and covered my head as whatever it was landed squarely on Barney's face and took him down. The letter went flying through the air. The gun fired wildly, the bullet grazing a tree nearby before pinging off into the darkness, but I didn't care about that as I helplessly watched the letter drift off on a gust of wind, flying over the treetops.

A guttural growl and a screech had me swiveling my attention back to Barney and whatever that thing was that was attacking him. Wait. Was that Felicity Bates's cat, Fluff?

Before I could ponder it further, another horrifying keen rang out, and Barney dropped the gun in favor of self-preservation. He had both hands on the cat now, trying to pry the fierce creature from his head.

Through the moonlight, I caught sight of the weapon a few feet away. This might be my only shot at escape. Trembling, I inched over and reached out to grab the gun, only to hear a voice behind me say, "Stop right there!"

28

Slowly, I turned to look over my shoulder and found another gun pointed in my general direction.

"Willa?" Gus said, squinting at me.

"Gus?" My voice sounded weak even to my own ears. Then again, my night hadn't exactly gone as planned. "How did you find me?"

She glanced over at Barney, still rolling around with Fluff's claws gouging his face, then shook her head. "What is it with you and cats, sis?"

Fluff stopped his attack suddenly and looked back at us, as if realizing for the first time that he wasn't alone. Then he gave one last, vicious swipe with his claw across Barney's battered nose and took off into the forest.

Barney Delaney rolled around on the ground, moaning and holding his head. "Help me! Willa tried to hit me with a shovel."

"What?" I wrinkled my nose in disbelief. At least the guy was consistent with his lies. "I did not—"

"Nice try, Delaney," Gus said, striding over to haul him to his feet. "Maybe next time you try to frame someone, don't use such a lame alibi."

"Lame?" Barney sounded outraged. "My alibi's rock solid."

"Really?" Gus spun him around and patted him down for more weapons before slapping a pair of handcuffs on him. "I can tell you for a fact it wasn't. See, I've suspected you all along. First was that diner receipt. Yes, you were there, but your order wasn't clocked in until five fifty-seven." Gus stepped back and crossed her arms. "Myrna's pretty darned quick. Meaning you would've had plenty of time that morning to kill Albert Schumer at five forty-five then rush back to the diner to get your food. It's just down the street. At least you were smart enough to park your car on the street, so you were already near the diner."

"That's not true. Not a word," Barney protested. "Yes, I was at the diner for a while before I ordered, but it took me a long time to decide what I wanted. Besides, I'm not the person you should be looking at for murder at all. The person you want is Nathan Anderson. There's even a witness who saw his car coming out of the post office parking lot around the time of the murder."

"Again, nice try," Gus countered, the smirk on her face saying she was enjoying nailing Barney to the wall. "But Myrna told me that you ordered the same thing you always do. No menu or deliberation needed. In fact, I was just on my way over to question you when I got a disturbance call from Mrs. McCarthy about some screeching in the woods behind her house. Didn't take long to follow all the earsplitting screeches from her driveway right here to you. I have no idea why you'd be out in the woods." Gus nodded at the shovel. "But I think that shovel will come in handy for evidence. I bet my next paycheck it was stolen from Nathan Anderson. The only thing I can't figure out is what Willa is doing out here too."

"Because he made me come," I said. "He held me at gunpoint and made me walk here. He said he was going to hit me with a shovel then throw me in the stream."

"That so?" Gus raised a brow. "Well, I can see how my sister might drive you to want to do that sometimes, but no one hurts my family."

Before I could say anything more, the sound of

snapping branches and approaching footsteps drew my attention. Next thing I knew, Striker and Pandora walked out of the forest and over to our little group. Several other cats emerged as well, ones I recognized from Elspeth's farm.

"Jeez, more cats?" Gus groused. She took Barney by the arm and shoved him forward toward the path and Striker. "And you. Where have you been? You were supposed to be covering my shift tonight so I could investigate. When I radioed in five minutes ago, though, they said you weren't at your desk, and now you end up here." Gus looked around. "With a bunch of cats. Seriously, what is up with all these cats?"

Pandora was busy rubbing her fur against my face and purring loudly. I scratched her behind the ears then glanced up to catch Striker's eye. He gave me an embarrassed smile then turned to face the wrath of Gus again.

"I guess they must have followed me," he said.

Gus looked at him as if she thought he was nuts. "Right. Okay, then, Pied Piper. I'm gonna traipse back through the woods to my cruiser with Delaney. Meet you at the station in ten. And no cats!" Gus led Barney off, reading him his rights as they went.

Striker came over to crouch beside me, his fingers

ruffling through Pandora's thick fur too. "So, Barney's the killer, huh? You okay, Chance?"

"Yes, on both counts." I took his hand to help me stand then brushed the leaves and muck off my pants. "Good thing Gus got here when she did too. He was going to knock me on the head and let me float away in the river."

"Well, I'm glad you're all right." He reached out to pluck a leaf from my hair, his fingertips grazing my cheek before falling away. Heat and awareness prickled my skin from his touch, and we both looked away, awkwardness ensuing. "And I know your sister isn't a believer in all the magical stuff around here, but she did more than lock up a killer tonight. Barney's a danger in more ways than one."

"He had the letter." I glanced up into the sky. "It floated off. We're going to need to come back here and look for it."

"We will. As soon as daylight hits."

I bent and picked up Pandora then walked out of the clearing with Striker by my side and the other cats swirling around our feet. "I hope it's not lost. Though maybe that would be for the best. Still, I'd like to make sure it's not floating around out there, able to get into the wrong hands. Though I have to say, a bit of old-world, not-so-commercial charm wouldn't be unwelcome around here. Barney was right about that."

Striker gave me a look over his shoulder. "Huh? So, you'd be fine with drawing your water from a well and using an outhouse again?"

"Okay. Maybe not that old-world." I chuckled and linked arms with him. "But there's something to be said for tiny-town treasures."

"Yeah, Chance." He patted my hand, his skin warm against mine. "There definitely is."

29

What a difference twenty-four hours made. I set down a tray of Earl Gray tea—no more ghostly visions tonight—and snickerdoodle cookies I'd picked up for dessert to go along with the pizza Striker had brought over and the breadsticks Gus picked up at the corner store.

"So, explain to me again exactly how you figured out Barney was guilty?" I said, taking the seat across the table from my sister. "I mean, I know you said you didn't believe his alibi."

Gus gnawed on a piece of breadstick while mulling this over. "Yeah, that's right. See, us *real* cops have a protocol we follow. First we get some suspects then check their alibis then follow up on clues. We don't just run around town, accusing people and getting almost killed in the woods like amateurs." She leveled a look at me, but then her eyes softened. "Anyway, I'd had my doubts about him all along, honestly. He just didn't act quite right during questioning, like he was hiding something. Turned out that something happened to be the fact he'd killed Albert."

"Yeah, but you told me he had an alibi. Seemed like you believed it then," I said.

"Nah, I just told you that so you wouldn't butt in and try to investigate him." She crunched off another bite of the breadstick. "Guess that didn't work."

Sipping my tea, I glanced over at Striker, who seemed quite engrossed in feeding Pandora pieces of pizza.

"Oh, you don't care for pepperoni, eh?" Striker said, chuckling as Pandora turned up her feline nose at his offering. He tossed the meat aside and tore off a piece of crust instead. The cat sat in his lap, preening and swishing her tail like the queen she envisioned herself to be. Striker held out the crust, and Pandora sniffed it before taking a tentative nibble.

Must be nice to have someone wait on you hand and foot like that. I did roll my eyes this time as Striker cooed and praised the cat for eating. "Ah, there's the ticket. You liked that, didn't you? Such a pretty girl. Yes. So pretty and smart and clever."

"Seriously, dude." Gus wrinkled her nose, giving him a disgruntled stare. "You carry on with that cat like it knows what you're saying."

I snorted. "She does have a point."

"Maybe she does understand me," Striker said, his expression turning defensive. "You ladies don't know."

Gus harrumphed. "Well, what I do know it that my sister here almost ruined everything last night. Speaking of explaining things, how about you tell me why you were out in the woods with a dangerous killer last night."

"Oh, well." I hid my fluster behind my mug of tea, taking a good long drink as I tried to come up with a plausible excuse that didn't involve talking to ghosts. My gaze landed on Pandora, who was now curled up in Striker's lap, purring loudly as she snoozed. Lucky girl.

After clearing my throat, I said, "I was looking for my cat."

As if in agreement, Pandora meowed in her sleep.

"That so." Gus sounded thoroughly unconvinced. "Then why'd she turn up with Striker later, sis?"

Crap. I met Striker's gaze with a help-me look.

His gray eyes widened slightly before he turned to

Gus with a frown. "I was looking for Pandora too. That's why I wasn't at my desk when you called in. I'd received a report right before that of a loose cat running in the street, and the description sounded exactly like Pandora here." He stroked the cat's head. "I didn't want anything to happen to Willa's pet, so of course I went right away to check it out."

"Of course you did." Gus's suspicious gaze darted between him and me. "What's going on with you two, huh? You guys moonlighting on investigations or something?"

"Uh, not exactly." Striker reached over and took my hand, which was resting atop the table. "We, um, we've gotten a lot closer over the past few weeks, and we're kind of more of a permanent thing now, I guess."

He gave me a hesitant look, and whatever reservations I'd had about our relationship caved. He was such a good guy—loyal, kind, smart, funny, brave. I'd be a fool to turn him away. I squeezed his fingers reassuringly. "Right. Yes. Striker and I are more of a permanent thing, Gus."

"Ugh." Gus made a face. "Please tell me you're not going to sit around and make googly eyes at each other all the time now. I need Striker to help out in Mystic Notch sometimes. I need him to be focused on cases, not wooing you, sis."

"I can do both," Striker said, gently setting the cat on the floor, then pushed to his feet to take our trash from dinner to the kitchen. Pandora scampered off toward the back door of the house. "I'm gifted that way."

I grinned as Striker winked at me. Gus groaned and stood as well. "That's it. I'm out of here." She wrapped half a dozen cookies in a napkin and shoved them in her pocket for later. "I'll give you guys some alone time so you can do... whatever it is you do."

"Thanks." I rose to walk my sister to the door. "What's going to happen with Barney and his shop?"

"He's currently being held in the county jail without bail. The judge was a personal friend of Albert Schumer's, so he'll go hard on the guy. My guess is Barney will sit in his cell until the trial. The case itself is pretty cut-and-dried, especially with the break-in to Nathan's shed and his shovel at the second crime scene. Your testimony will help too, him threatening to bash your head in with it then trying to frame Nathan for the murder. You'll still testify, right?"

"Yep. Absolutely."

"Good." Gus started out the door then stopped. "Oh, and about Barney's shop, I heard his niece will be coming from Salem to take over the place."

"Is that so?" Striker said, joining us. He gave me an uneasy glance.

"Well, I'm off." Gus waved as she walked out the door. "You two have fun. Don't do anything I wouldn't do."

Alone at last, Striker and I settled on the sofa with our mugs of tea and a plate of cookies. I still couldn't seem to shake my niggling unease about Albert's murder. "What about Albert's letter? We searched the entire area but didn't find it."

"I know. We can look some more later," he said around a bite of snickerdoodle. "If we're lucky, it fell in the stream and is lost for good. Too many people want to get their wicked little hands on it."

I shuddered and cuddled into his side. His arm came around my shoulders, warm and comforting. My gaze settled on the paperweight on the table. I half expected to see some ghastly vision of death or destruction, but all that shone back at me was my own reflection. Funny, but it was sort of disappointing after all the excitement of the last few days. Still, maybe it would be better if all those visions and clues in the glass globe had been nothing more than fantasies cooked up in my own imagination, as Gus would suggest. At least it would mean there was no new mystery to solve.

Pandora hopped up on the couch and nestled in between us. My worries about the letter melted away. Things felt good, right. The letter had blown away, probably stuck in a tree or decaying in the dirt by now. I was almost certain that Mystic Notch would remain as pleasant as it had always been for a long, long time.

30

Later that night...

DEEP in the woods of Mystic Notch, Fluff sat hunched over the small stream, the full moon glimmering off its silvery waters.

Things had not turned out the way he'd wanted, but he could make it right. His human was counting on him, and he had to redeem himself.

It wasn't his fault the letter had been lost. That dimwit, Barney Delaney, should have just handed it over. But no, he'd clung onto it and then tossed it in the air. And that stupid Willa Chance—her presence had messed everything up.

Pandora and the other cats thought they were so superior. He'd show them. Bunch of ingrates. Not once had they even tried to make friends with him. Not that he cared. He was a loner. And besides, he was much more powerful than any of them, even that loudmouth, Inkspot.

They'd see. Once things turned around in Mystic Notch, Fluff would have his own band of cats. Then Pandora, Inkspot, and the others would be sorry. And Hope would wish she'd come over to his side.

Fluff hunkered down, staring into the dark water. The sounds of it lapping against the stones in the brook mingled with the buzzing of nighttime insects.

Fluff grumbled to himself then jerked in surprise as something came floating down the stream—pale and soggy. He dipped a paw into the icy waters and skewered the object with his claw, dragging it out.

A half piece of paper, torn down the middle. It was waterlogged, its smudged black ink smearing all over it. Carefully, Fluff batted the paper open with his paw. This was it, the list of ingredients. Well, only half a list, to be exact. But one could still make out some of the words. Maybe this would still be of use to his human.

Fluff gently put the list in his mouth and ran toward the Bates Mansion.

****

Sign up for my newsletter and get my latest releases at the lowest discount price, plus I'll send you a link for a free download of a book in one of my other series: https://mystic_notch.gr8.com/

Books in the Mystic Notch series:

Ghostly Paws
A Spirited Tail
A Mew To A Kill
Paws and Effect
Probable Paws
A Whisker of a Doubt
Wrong Side of the Claw

If you want to receive a text message on your cell

phone when I have a new release, text COZYMYSTERY to 88202 (sorry, this only works for US cell phones!)

Join my readers group on Facebook: https://www.facebook.com/groups/ldobbsreaders

MORE BOOKS BY LEIGHANN DOBBS:

Cozy Mysteries

Silver Hollow

Paranormal Cozy Mystery Series

***

A Spell of Trouble (Book 1)

Spell Disaster (Book 2)

Nothing to Croak About (Book 3)

Cry Wolf (Book 4)

Shear Magic (Book 5)

Blackmoore Sisters

Cozy Mystery Series

* * *

Dead Wrong

Dead & Buried

Dead Tide

Buried Secrets

Deadly Intentions

A Grave Mistake

Spell Found

Fatal Fortune

Hidden Secrets

Oyster Cove Guesthouse

Cat Cozy Mystery Series

***

A Twist in the Tail

A Whisker in the Dark

A Purrfect Alibi

Mystic Notch

Cat Cozy Mystery Series

* * *

Ghostly Paws

A Spirited Tail

A Mew To A Kill

Paws and Effect

Probable Paws

Whisker of a Doubt

Wrong Side of the Claw

Oyster Cove Guesthouse

Cat Cozy Mystery Series

***

A Twist in the Tail

A Whisker in the Dark

Kate Diamond Mystery Adventures

***

Hidden Agemda (Book 1)

Ancient Hiss Story (Book 2)

Heist Society (Book 3)

Mooseamuck Island

Cozy Mystery Series

* * *

A Zen For Murder

A Crabby Killer

A Treacherous Treasure

Lexy Baker

Cozy Mystery Series

* * *

Lexy Baker Cozy Mystery Series Boxed Set Vol 1 (Books 1-4)

Or buy the books separately:

Killer Cupcakes

Dying For Danish

Murder, Money and Marzipan

3 Bodies and a Biscotti

Brownies, Bodies & Bad Guys

Bake, Battle & Roll

Wedded Blintz

Scones, Skulls & Scams

Ice Cream Murder

Mummified Meringues

Brutal Brulee (Novella)

No Scone Unturned

Cream Puff Killer

Never Say Pie

Lady Katherine Regency Mysteries

***

An Invitation to Murder (Book 1)

The Baffling Burglaries of Bath (Book 2)

Murder at the Ice Ball (Book 3)

A Murderous Affair (Book 4)

Hazel Martin Historical Mystery Series

***

Murder at Lowry House (book 1)

Murder by Misunderstanding (book 2)

Sam Mason Mysteries

(As L. A. Dobbs)

***

Telling Lies (Book 1)

Keeping Secrets (Book 2)

Exposing Truths (Book 3)

Betraying Trust (Book 4)

Killing Dreams (Book 5)

Romantic Comedy

***

Corporate Chaos Series

In Over Her Head (book 1)

Can't Stand the Heat (book 2)

What Goes Around Comes Around (book 3)

Careful What You Wish For (4)

Contemporary Romance

***

Reluctant Romance

Sweet Romance (Written As Annie Dobbs)

Firefly Inn Series

***

Another Chance (Book 1)

Another Wish (Book 2)

Hometown Hearts Series

***

No Getting Over You (Book 1)

A Change of Heart (Book 2)

Sweet Mountain Billionaires

***

Jaded Billionaire (Book 1)

A Billion Reasons Not To Fall In Love (Book 2)

Regency Romance

* * *

Scandals and Spies Series:

Kissing The Enemy

Deceiving the Duke

Tempting the Rival

Charming the Spy

Pursuing the Traitor

Captivating the Captain